TOM'S MIDNIGHT GARDEN

A GRAPHIC ADAPTATION OF
THE PHILIPPA PEARCE CLASSIC

BY EDITH

GREENWILLOW BOOKS, *An Imprint of* HarperCollins*Publishers*

For Kayla, Chloe and Olivia.

Edith

"One might be under the impression that
gardens lend themselves easily as settings
for novels, but it's more than that—in fact
novels and gardens are born of the same
process. To write a story is to sow a seed."

Michel Foucault (Les Hétérotopies)

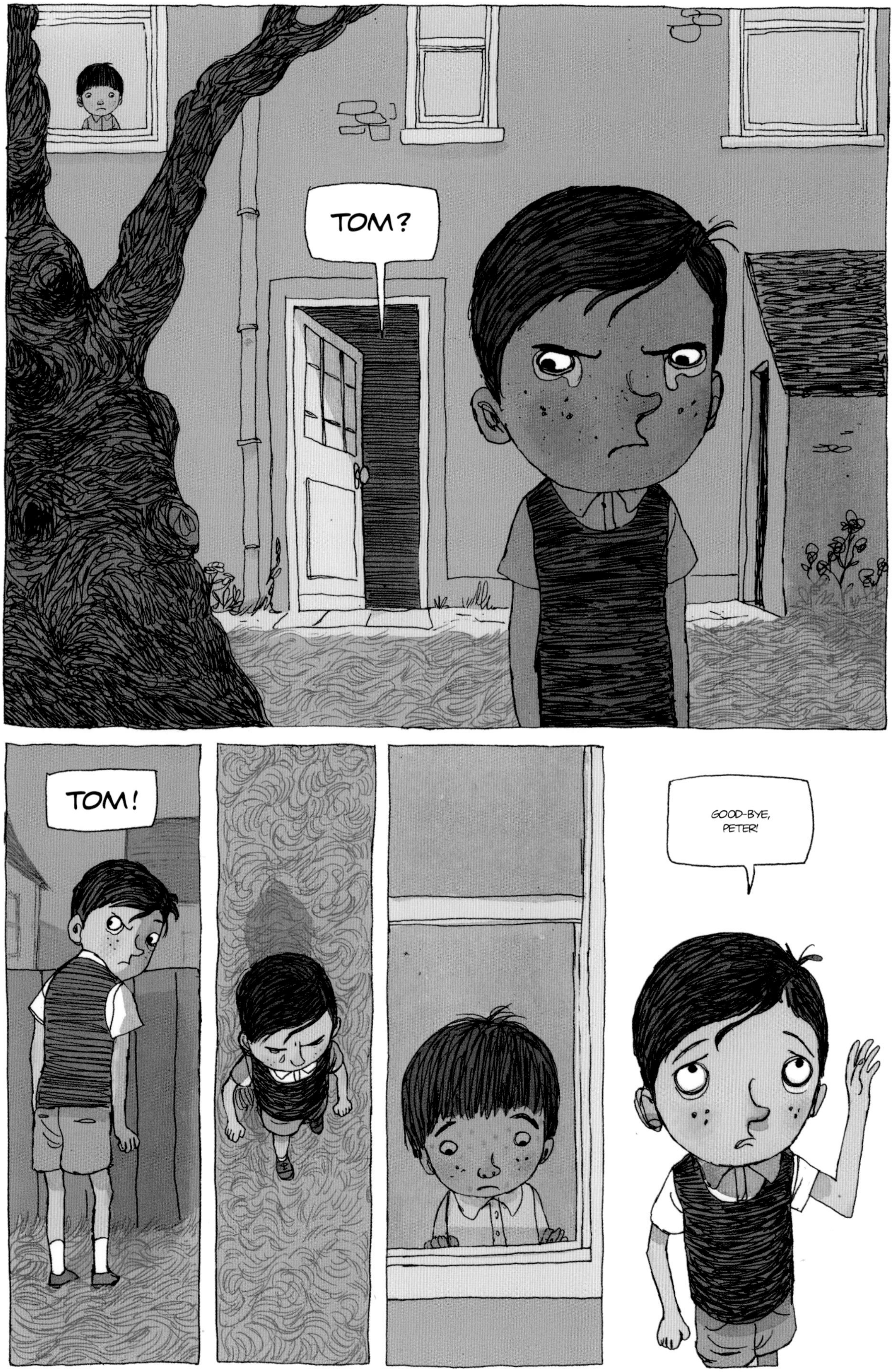
TOM?
TOM!
GOOD-BYE, PETER!

IT'S NOT NICE FOR US EITHER, TOM.

YOUR FATHER AND I WILL MISS YOU, AND SO WILL PETER. PETER'S NOT HAVING A NICE TIME, ANYWAY, WITH MEASLES.

I DIDN'T SAY YOU'D ALL BE HAVING A NICE TIME WITHOUT ME . . .

ALL I SAID WAS . . .

HUSH!

TOM, DEAR TOM, REMEMBER THAT YOU WILL BE A VISITOR, AND DO TRY — OH, WHAT CAN I SAY? — TRY TO BE GOOD.

GIVE MY LOVE TO GWEN, ALAN,

AND TELL HER HOW GRATEFUL WE ARE TO YOU BOTH FOR TAKING TOM OFF AT SUCH SHORT NOTICE. IT'S VERY KIND OF YOU.

ISN'T IT, TOM?

VERY KIND.

I'D RATHER HAVE HAD MEASLES WITH PETER — MUCH RATHER!

I AM SORRY — SPOILING THE BEGINNING OF YOUR SUMMER HOLIDAYS LIKE THIS!

ANYWAY . . .

I HOPE WE GET ON REASONABLY WELL.

TOOT!
TOOT!

TOM!

MEASLES! POOR PETER . . .

AND YOU'LL HAVE TO STAY IN QUARANTINE UNTIL WE KNOW IF YOU'VE CAUGHT IT OR NOT . . .

IN A FORTNIGHT WE'LL KNOW FOR SURE.

THE CLOCK BELONGS TO OLD MRS. BARTHOLOMEW UPSTAIRS. SHE'S RATHER PARTICULAR ABOUT IT.

DON'T TOUCH IT, TOM.

IF MRS. BARTHOLOMEW'S PARTICULAR ABOUT HER CLOCK, WHY DOESN'T SHE HAVE IT UPSTAIRS WITH HER?

BECAUSE THE CLOCK IS SCREWED TO THE WALL AT THE BACK, AND THE SCREWS HAVE RUSTED IN.

COME AWAY FROM IT, DO, TOM. COME UP TO TEA.

IN ANY CASE, IT KEEPS GOOD TIME BUT SELDOM CHOOSES TO STRIKE THE RIGHT HOUR.

THIS IS YOUR ROOM, TOM DEAR. I'VE PUT FLOWERS IN IT, AND BOOKS FOR YOU TO READ.

BUT THERE ARE BARS ACROSS THE WINDOW! THIS IS A NURSERY! I'M NOT A BABY!

OF COURSE NOT — OF COURSE NOT! IT'S NOTHING TO DO WITH YOU, TOM. THIS WINDOW HAD BARS ACROSS IT WHEN WE CAME.

THE BATHROOM WINDOW HAD TOO, FOR THAT MATTER.

TEA WILL BE READY IN FIVE MINUTES. I'VE MADE SCONES AND THERE'S HOMEMADE STRAWBERRY JAM . . .

I'LL SPOIL YOU FOR FOOD WHILE YOU'RE WITH US.

DEAR PETER, I HOPE YOUR MEASLES ARE BETTER. THIS IS A PICTURE OF THE CATHEDRAL TOWER AT ELY. WE CAME THROUGH ELY, BUT UNCLE ALAN WOULDN'T LET ME GO UP THE TOWER. HE JUST LET ME BUY THIS POSTCARD . . .

THE HOUSE HERE IS FLATS AND THERE ISN'T ANY GARDEN. MY BEDROOM WINDOW HAS BARS, BUT AUNT GWEN SAYS IT'S A MISTAKE.

THE FOOD IS GOOD. TOM

DONG !

DONG !

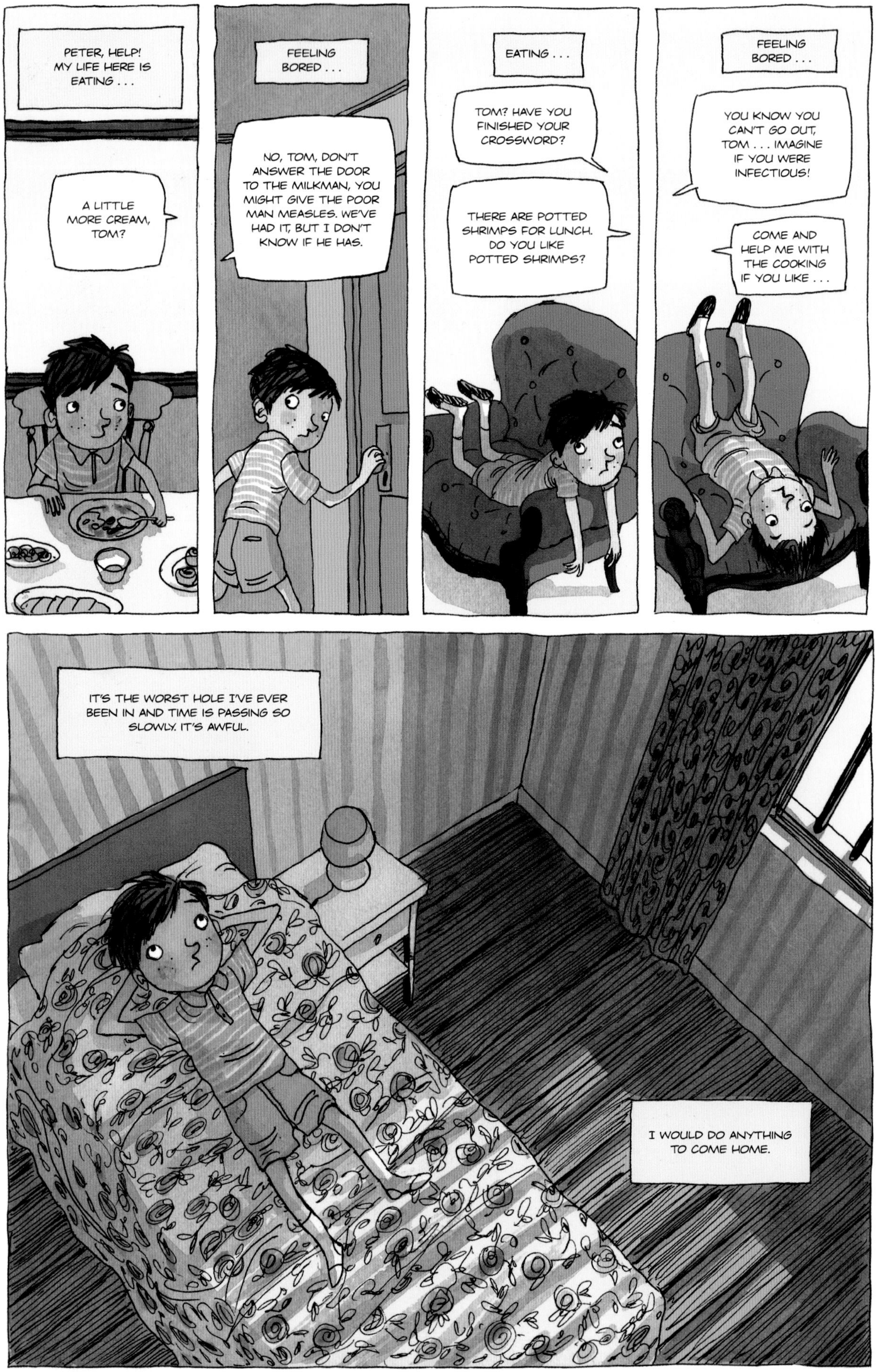
PETER, HELP! MY LIFE HERE IS EATING . . .
A LITTLE MORE CREAM, TOM?
FEELING BORED . . .
NO, TOM, DON'T ANSWER THE DOOR TO THE MILKMAN, YOU MIGHT GIVE THE POOR MAN MEASLES. WE'VE HAD IT, BUT I DON'T KNOW IF HE HAS.
EATING . . .
TOM? HAVE YOU FINISHED YOUR CROSSWORD?
THERE ARE POTTED SHRIMPS FOR LUNCH. DO YOU LIKE POTTED SHRIMPS?
FEELING BORED . . .
YOU KNOW YOU CAN'T GO OUT, TOM . . . IMAGINE IF YOU WERE INFECTIOUS!
COME AND HELP ME WITH THE COOKING IF YOU LIKE . . .
IT'S THE WORST HOLE I'VE EVER BEEN IN AND TIME IS PASSING SO SLOWLY. IT'S AWFUL.
I WOULD DO ANYTHING TO COME HOME.

AT NIGHT, I CAN'T GET TO SLEEP.

I TRY READING, BUT ALL I HAVE IS A.G.'S SCHOOLGIRL STORIES . . .

SOMETIMES I GET UP, AND GO TO THE PANTRY, JUST TO DO SOMETHING.

LAST NIGHT, U.A. FOUND ME THERE. IT MUST HAVE BEEN LATE. A.G. WAS MOST UPSET. SHE THOUGHT I WAS STILL HUNGRY. U.A. GAVE ME A LECTURE . . .

TOM, THERE MUST BE NO MORE OF THIS. YOU ARE NOT TO PUT THE LIGHT ON AGAIN ONCE IT HAS BEEN PUT OUT; NOR, EQUALLY, ARE YOU TO GET OUT OF BED.

NOT EVEN TO GET UP IN THE MORNING?

OF COURSE, THAT'S DIFFERENT. DON'T BE SILLY, TOM. BUT YOU ARE NOT TO GET UP OTHERWISE.

BUT, UNCLE ALAN, I DON'T SLEEP!

ALL CHILDREN SLEEP!

U.A. SAYS I HAVE TO BE IN BED FROM NINE O'CLOCK AT NIGHT AND BE ASLEEP FOR TEN HOURS. HE MADE ME PROMISE TO OBSERVE THEIR WISHES.

DONGGG !

DONG ! DONGG! DONG ! DONG ! DONG ! DONG !

TEN! ELEVEN! TWELVE! MIDNIGHT, AND I'M STILL NOT ASLEEP . . .

DONG !

THIRTEEN?!

PETER, I HAD TO KNOW WHAT TIME THE CLOCK FINGERS WOULD BE SHOWING WHEN IT STRUCK THIRTEEN . . .

I DECIDED TO GO AND LOOK.

IT WAS
TOO DARK.
I COULDN'T
SEE THE
CLOCK FACE.

I SAW THAT
MOONBEAMS WERE
SHINING THROUGH
THE WINDOW OF THE
BACK DOOR.

I THOUGHT IF I OPENED
THE DOOR, PERHAPS IT
WOULD LET IN ENOUGH
LIGHT TO READ THE
CLOCK FACE.

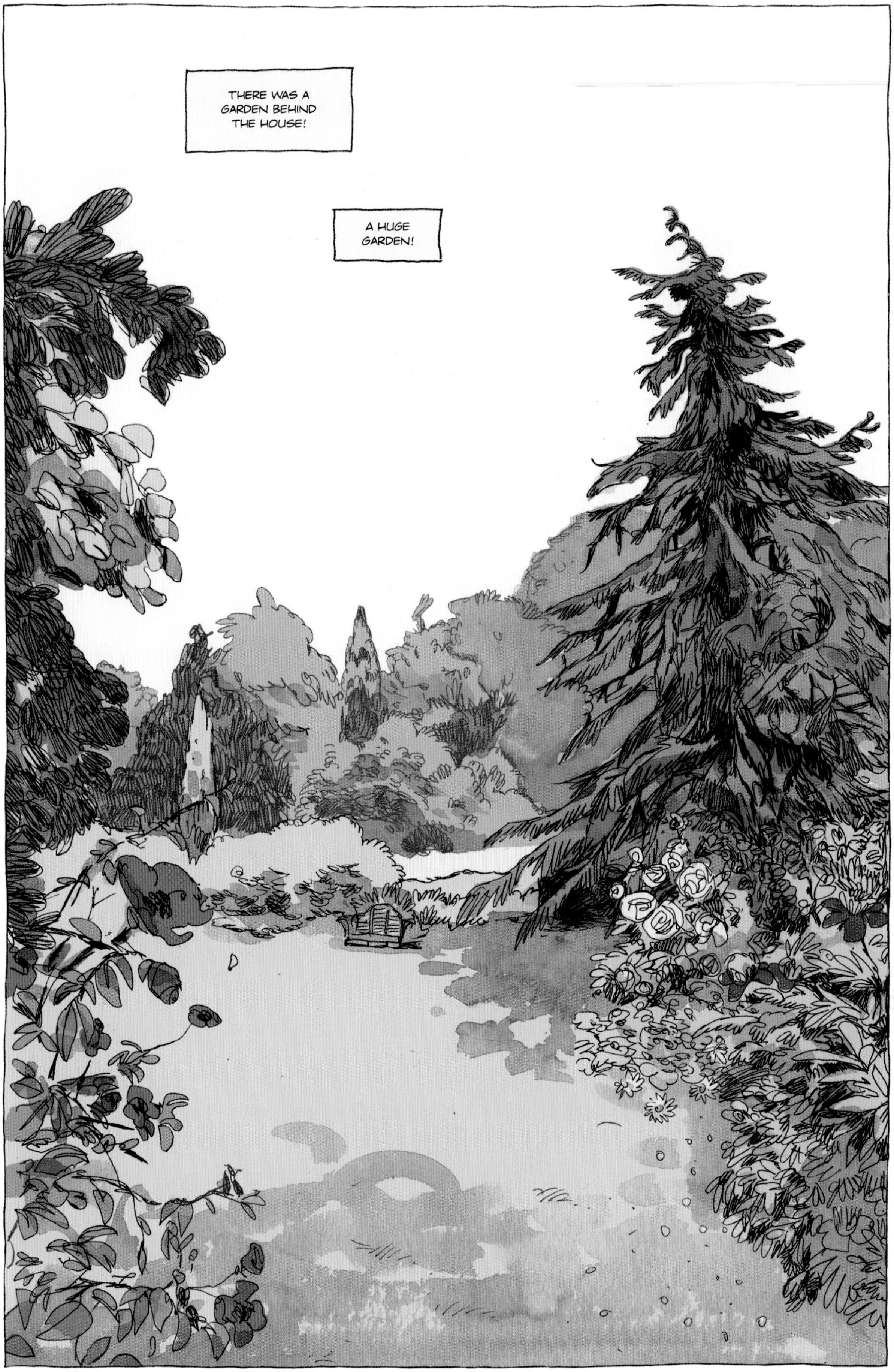
THERE WAS A GARDEN BEHIND THE HOUSE!
A HUGE GARDEN!

IT'S NOT WORTH YOUR WHILE GOING OUT AT THE BACK, TOM.

A SORT OF BACK-YARD, VERY POKY, WITH RUBBISH BINS. REALLY, THERE'S NOTHING TO SEE.

I DIDN'T STAY LONG.
I DIDN'T WANT TO RISK
U.A. AND A.G. NOTICING
I WAS MISSING.

12

MADAM . . .

. . . I'VE LIT THE FIRE IN THE PARLOR.

THEN . . .

. . . SOMETHING VERY CURIOUS HAPPENED.

I SHALL GO BACK DOWN TOMORROW.

DO YOU BELIEVE THAT LYING IS WRONG?

OH, TOM! ALWAYS!

I MEAN, DO YOU THINK THAT SOME SPECIAL LIES MIGHT BE RIGHT, SOMETIMES?

I SUPPOSE, TOM, YOU ARE THINKING OF WHAT ARE COMMONLY KNOWN AS WHITE LIES?

I DON'T THINK SO, EXACTLY. AT LEAST, I MEAN — WELL, SOMEONE BEING KEPT IN THE DARK ABOUT SOMETHING HE'D ENJOY, BECAUSE SOME OTHER PEOPLE DIDN'T WANT TO TELL HIM ABOUT IT. I MEAN, SUPPOSING THE OTHER PEOPLE WENT SO FAR AS TO SAY THE THING JUST WASN'T THERE, IN ORDER NOT TO HAVE THE BOTHER OF THE FIRST PERSON USING IT.

WHAT KIND OF THING WAS IT THE SECOND PEOPLE DIDN'T WANT THE FIRST PEOPLE TO KNOW ABOUT AND USE?

FIRST PERSON, NOT FIRST PEOPLE. AND THE THING WAS — WELL —

A HOT-WATER BOTTLE, SAY?

NO, MORE LIKE . . .

IT DOESN'T REALLY MATTER WHAT THE THING IS, GWEN. IF I UNDERSTAND TOM, THE POINT IS THAT SOME PERSON OR PERSONS WERE LYING SIMPLY FOR THEIR OWN CONVENIENCE, AND TO THE HARM OF ANOTHER PERSON OR PERSONS. IS THAT SO, TOM?

YES. I JUST WONDERED IF YOU THOUGHT THAT KIND OF LIE MIGHT BE RIGHT.

OF ALL POSSIBLE FORMS OF LYING, THAT IS SURELY THE LEAST JUSTIFIABLE.

I AM SURPRISED, TOM, THAT YOU SHOULD HAVE ANY DOUBTS ABOUT IT.

NEVER MIND, TOM. UNCLE ALAN HAS A VERY HIGHLY DEVELOPED SENSE OF RIGHT AND WRONG. HE SAYS SO HIMSELF. YOU WILL HAVE ONE TOO, I'M SURE, WHEN YOU GROW UP.

I HAVE ONE NOW!

IT'S OTHER PEOPLE WHO HAVEN'T!

AUNT GWEN.

YES, TOM?

IT WAS KIND OF YOU TO PUT FLOWERS IN MY BEDROOM WHEN I CAME.

TOM, DEAR, I DIDN'T KNOW YOU'D NOTICED THEM!

HAD YOU TO BUY THEM?

YES, BUT YOU MUSTN'T BOTHER ABOUT THAT.

IT WOULD HAVE BEEN EASIER FOR YOU IF YOU'D BEEN ABLE TO GET FLOWERS FROM A GARDEN OF YOUR OWN.

YES, BUT THERE ISN'T A GARDEN TO THIS HOUSE, OF COURSE.

NO?

WHAT DO YOU MEAN BY "NO," TOM?

I MEANT, WHAT A PITY! WOULDN'T IT BE NICE IF THERE WERE A GARDEN AT THE BACK OF THE HOUSE — WITH A LAWN AND TREES AND FLOWERS AND EVEN A GREENHOUSE?

IT WOULD BE NICE, TOO, IF WE HAD WINGS AND COULD FLY, TOM.

SUPPOSE YOU COULD WALK OUT OF THE DOOR AT THE BACK THIS VERY MINUTE, AUNT GWEN — THIS VERY MINUTE — AND WALK ON TO A LAWN AND CUT HYACINTHS FROM THE FLOWER BEDS ON THAT LAWN?

FLOWER BEDS SHAPED LIKE THE QUARTERS OF AN ORANGE?

TO BEGIN WITH, TOM, I SHOULD BE VERY SURPRISED INDEED IF YOU PICKED ME A HYACINTH FROM ANYWHERE OUTSIDE, NOW.

OH?

HYACINTHS DON'T FLOWER EVEN OUT OF DOORS AT THIS TIME OF YEAR — IT'S TOO LATE IN THE SUMMER. SEE WHAT YOUR ROMANCING HAS LED YOU INTO!

BUT I'VE S-SEEN HYACINTHS FLOWERING OUT OF DOORS, AT JUST THIS TIME OF YEAR!

NO, TOM, YOU CAN'T HAVE. THEY'RE QUITE OVER.

I'M GOING DOWNSTAIRS, IF YOU DON'T MIND.

WHAT FOR, TOM?

NOTHING SPECIAL. I WON'T DO ANYTHING WRONG.

DON'T GO THIS MORNING. THIS IS THE MORNING THAT MRS. BARTHOLOMEW ALWAYS GOES DOWNSTAIRS TO WIND THE GRANDFATHER CLOCK.

DON'T BE A FOOL! IT'S THERE, I TELL YOU! THE GARDEN'S THERE!

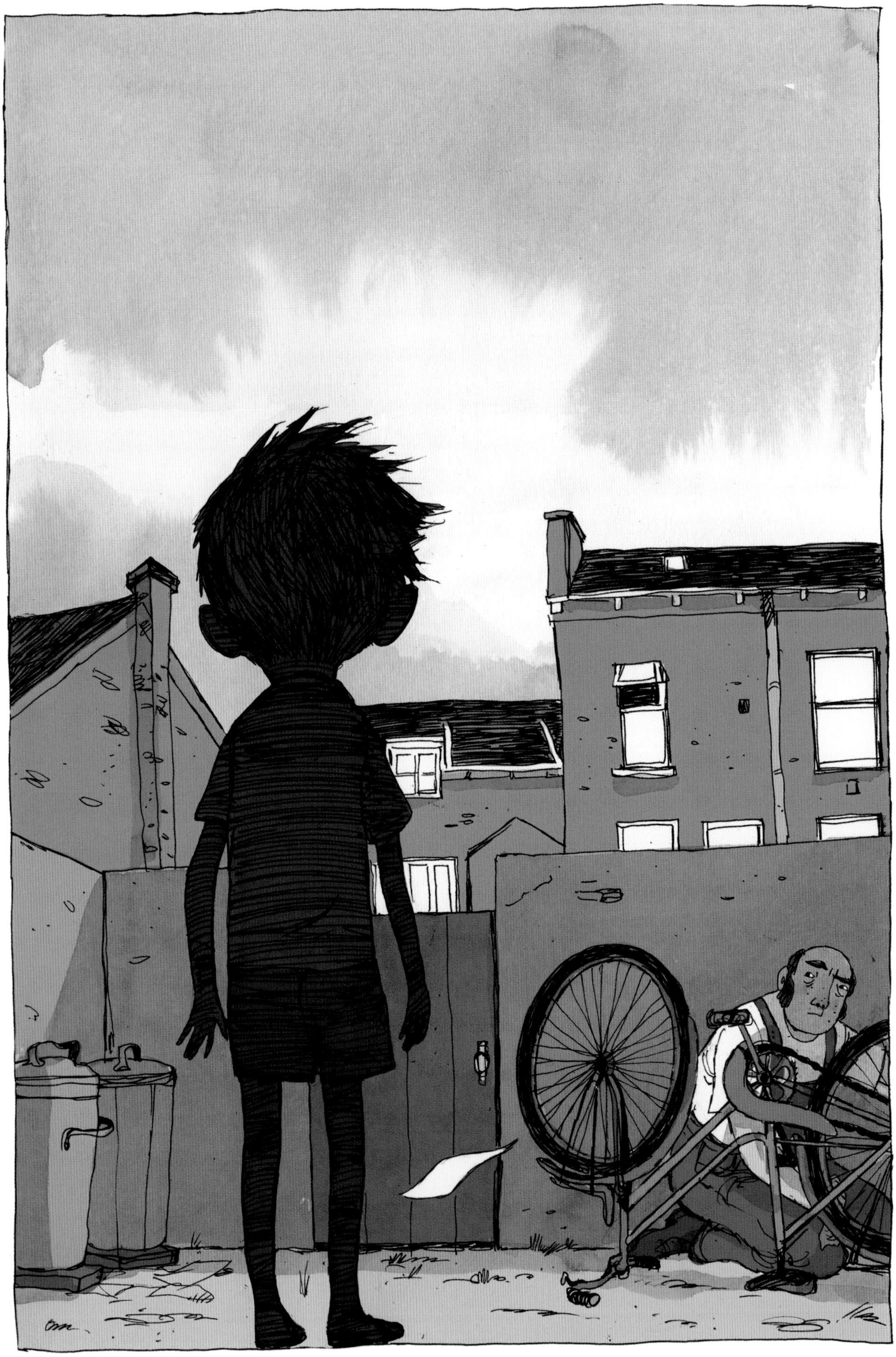

HALLO! WHO ARE YOU?

OH, I KNOW — YOU'RE THE BOY FROM THE FIRST FLOOR FRONT — THE KITSONS'.

A BIT DULL FOR YOU HERE, ISN'T IT?

YES. DO YOU LIVE IN THE GROUND FLOOR BACK FLAT?

YES.

DO YOU HAVE A MAID THAT LIGHTS YOUR FIRE FOR YOU?

A WHAT?

AND YOU DON'T — YOU DON'T HAVE A GARDEN, EITHER?

HERE, I SAY! WHAT ON EARTH'S THE MATTER?

LEAVE ME ALONE!

WAIT!

WAIT A MINUTE!

LISTEN!

I THOUGHT SO.

IT'S OLD MA BARTHOLOMEW, COMING TO WIND UP HER PRECIOUS CLOCK. YOU DON'T WANT TO RUN INTO HER. THERE'VE NEVER BEEN CHILDREN HERE, AND SHE MIGHT NOT LIKE IT.

WHAT'S BITTEN YOU NOW?

NOTHING. THANK YOU FOR WARNING ME ABOUT MRS. BARTHOLOMEW. GOOD-BYE.

DEAR PETER, TONIGHT I MEAN TO CLIMB INTO THE NEXT-DOOR GARDEN AND EXAMINE THE YEW TREE THERE BECAUSE — SURELY — IT WAS ONE OF THE TREES THAT I SAW IN **THE** GARDEN.

I MUST SOLVE THIS MYSTERY.

BURN AFTER READING!

B.A.R.

STRIKING HOURS AND HOURS
THAT DON'T EXIST!
I ONLY HOPE IT'S KEEPING
MRS. BARTHOLOMEW AWAKE, TOO.

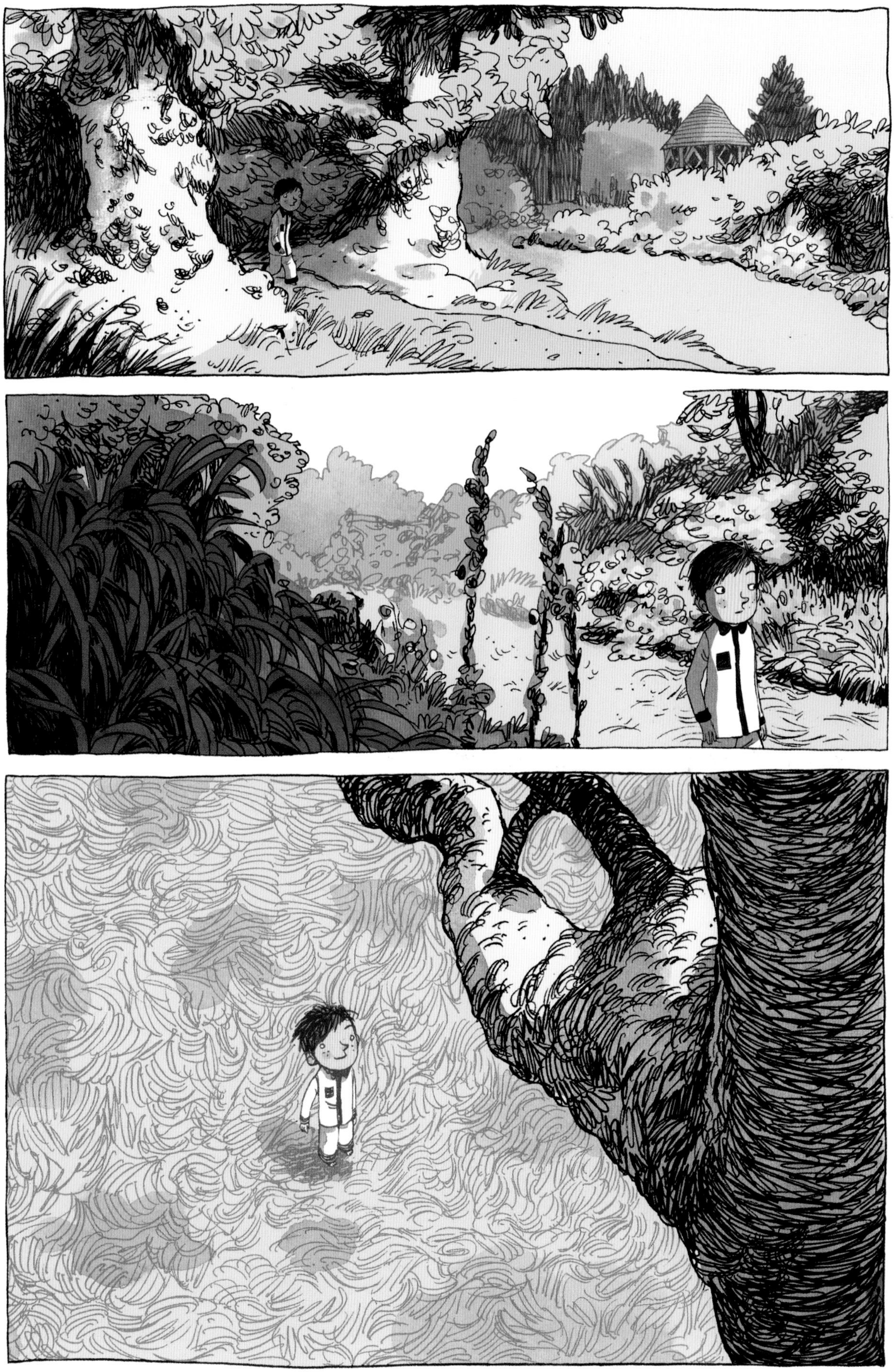

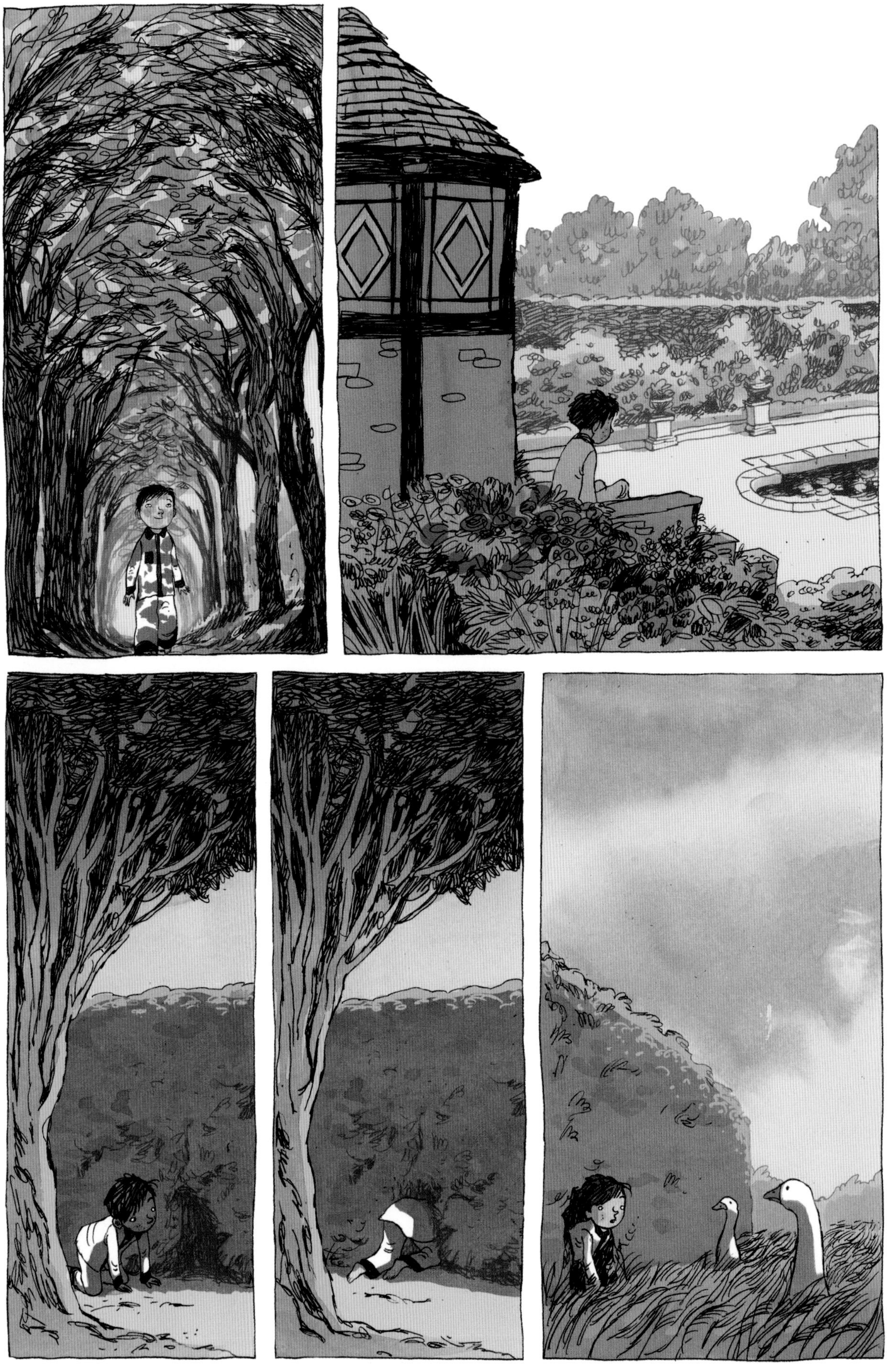

TO OBERON, KING OF FAIRIES.

CLACK!

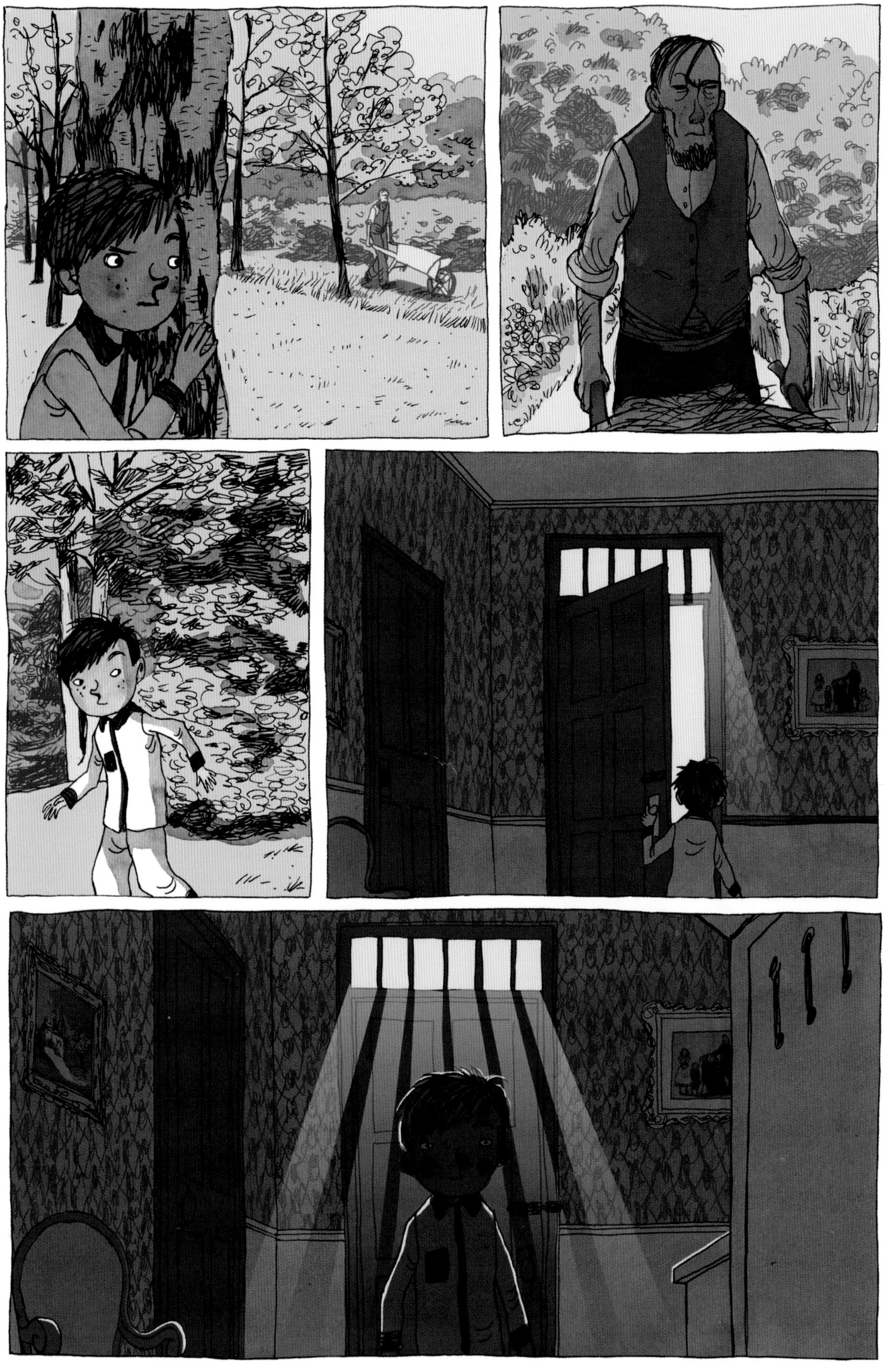

WHEN I WENT BACK INTO THE FLAT, I WENT INTO THE KITCHEN TO CONSULT THE CLOCK THERE.

?

PETER, IT WAS STILL ONLY A FEW MINUTES PAST MIDNIGHT!

IF THAT GRANDFATHER CLOCK STRIKES ONE IN ANYTHING LIKE THE WAY IT'S JUST STRUCK TWELVE — ON AND ON AND ON — THEN I'LL GO UPSTAIRS AND KNOCK MRS. BARTHOLOMEW UP AND COMPLAIN. SHE NEEDN'T THINK I'M FRIGHTENED OF HER.

PETER. AT FIRST I USED
TO BE AFRAID THE GARDEN
WOULD DISAPPEAR. BUT NO.

I SLIP DOWN THERE
EVERY NIGHT.

AND EVERY NIGHT
IT'S THERE.

THE PEOPLE IN THE GARDEN CAN'T SEE ME.

AND . . . I DON'T KNOW HOW TO EXPLAIN IT . . . IT'S AS IF I DON'T WEIGH A THING.

I CAN'T OPEN ANY OF THE DOORS IN THE GARDEN BY PUSHING WITH MY HAND. I'M GOING TO WAIT FOR THE GARDENER TO OPEN ONE AND FOLLOW AT HIS HEELS . . .

IT DIDN'T WORK. HE SHUT THE DOOR TOO QUICKLY.

BUT I DISCOVERED SOMETHING INCREDIBLE . . .

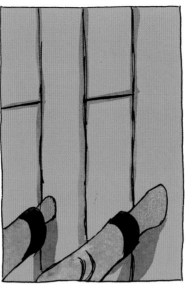

FOR ALL GOOD THINGS I THANK THE LORD; AND MAY HE KEEP ME FROM ALL THE WORKS OF THE DEVIL THAT HE HURT ME NOT.

TO GO BACK, I GOT INTO THE WHEELBARROW . . .

. . . BECAUSE THE FEELING OF GOING THROUGH A SHUT DOOR WAS NOT AT ALL ENJOYABLE.

THE DAY BEFORE
YESTERDAY,
SOMETHING TERRIBLE
HAPPENED . . .

CRACK!

OH!

. . . SOMEONE
CRIED OUT.

K.KRAA BAAAAAM

BUT WHEN I CAME BACK THE FOLLOWING NIGHT . . .

. . . NOT UNLESS YOU PUT THE CLOCK BACK.

WHAT CLOCK?

WHAT DID YOU SAY, TOM?

YOU SAID A TREE COULD NOT BE LYING FALLEN AT ONE TIME, AND THEN BE STANDING UP AGAIN AS IT WAS BEFORE IT FELL, UNLESS YOU PUT THE CLOCK BACK. WHAT CLOCK?

OH, NO PARTICULAR CLOCK. IT'S JUST A SAYING, TOM, "TO PUT THE CLOCK BACK." IT MEANS, TO HAVE THE PAST AGAIN, AND NO ONE CAN HAVE THAT. TIME ISN'T LIKE THAT.

WHAT **IS** TIME LIKE, UNCLE ALAN?

TOM, YOU SHOULDN'T ALWAYS BE ASKING SUCH VERY ODD QUESTIONS OF YOUR UNCLE. HE'S TIRED AFTER HIS DAY'S WORK.

NO, NO, GWEN. A CHILD'S QUESTIONS SHOULD CERTAINLY BE ANSWERED. ALL I WOULD OBJECT TO TOM'S QUESTIONS IS THEIR LACK OF CONNECTION, AND SOMETIMES OF SERIOUSNESS, TOO. LOOK AT HIS FIRST QUESTION: HE ASKED WHETHER IT WOULD BE POSSIBLE TO GO THROUGH A DOOR — HE ACTUALLY ASKED HOW IT WOULD BE POSSIBLE!

WELL! WELL, THAT SEEMS A VERY SENSIBLE IDEA — SO SENSIBLE THAT IT'S ALMOST SILLY!

NOT WHEN THE DOOR IS SHUT . . . THEN HE WENT ON TO ASK ABOUT INVISIBILITY.

AND FINALLY, WE HAVE THIS QUESTION ABOUT A TREE'S BEING ABLE TO LIE FALLEN ONE DAY, AND THEN, ON THE NEXT DAY, AGAINST ALL THE KNOWN LAWS OF NATURE —

IT WAS A DREAM! JUST A QUEER DREAM, WASN'T IT, TOM?

NO, IT WASN'T! IT WAS REAL!

INDEED! TELL US WHERE, TOM, AND WHEN.

NO, TOM MUSTN'T SPEAK AGAIN UNTIL HE'S FINISHED HIS LETTER TO PETER, NOR BE INTERRUPTED.

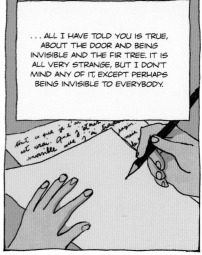

. . . ALL I HAVE TOLD YOU IS TRUE, ABOUT THE DOOR AND BEING INVISIBLE AND THE FIR TREE. IT IS ALL VERY STRANGE, BUT I DON'T MIND ANY OF IT, EXCEPT PERHAPS BEING INVISIBLE TO EVERYBODY.

FOR INSTANCE, THERE ARE THREE BOYS THAT HAVE COME INTO THE GARDEN. THEIR NAMES ARE HUBERT AND JAMES AND EDGAR. EDGAR IS ABOUT MY AGE, BUT I THINK I WOULD LIKE JAMES BETTER. THERE IS A GIRL WHO TAGS ROUND AFTER THEM. SHE IS VERY YOUNG AND IS CALLED HATTY OR SOMETHING . . .

IT'S USELESS TO WRITE AT LENGTH TO ANYONE RECOVERING FROM MEASLES. AFTER MEASLES, THE PATIENT HAS TO BE PARTICULARLY CAREFUL NOT TO STRAIN HIS EYES BY OVERUSE.

IF TOM'S LETTER IS TOO LONG FOR PETER, THEN NO DOUBT HIS MOTHER WILL READ IT ALOUD TO HIM.

A.G. TOLD ME I WOULD BE HERE FOR TEN MORE DAYS. BUT SUDDENLY I DON'T WANT TO GO HOME . . .

I EVEN WISH I HAD THE MEASLES SO I COULD STAY A BIT LONGER. I DON'T WANT TO LEAVE THE GARDEN.

ESPECIALLY BECAUSE SOMETHING ELSE HAS HAPPENED . . .

LET'S ALL RUN FROM HATTY!

AAAH . . .

YOU JUGGINS — YOU SILLY LITTLE JUGGINS, YOU!

YOU SHOULD LOOK WHERE YOU'RE GOING! I CAN'T HELP YOU — I'M OFF WITH THE OTHERS!

OH, JAMES, WHAT WILL AUNT SAY?

COO-EEE!

JAMES!

JAMES!

WE WERE ONLY TOLD NOT TO PICK ANY. COME ON, LADS! SHAKE THE TREE AND MAKE THEM FALL!

SPYING!

GIVE ME AN APPLE, PLEASE.

DON'T LEAVE THE CORE ON THE LAWN, HATTY, OR YOU'LL GET YOURSELF INTO TROUBLE, AND US TOO, PERHAPS.

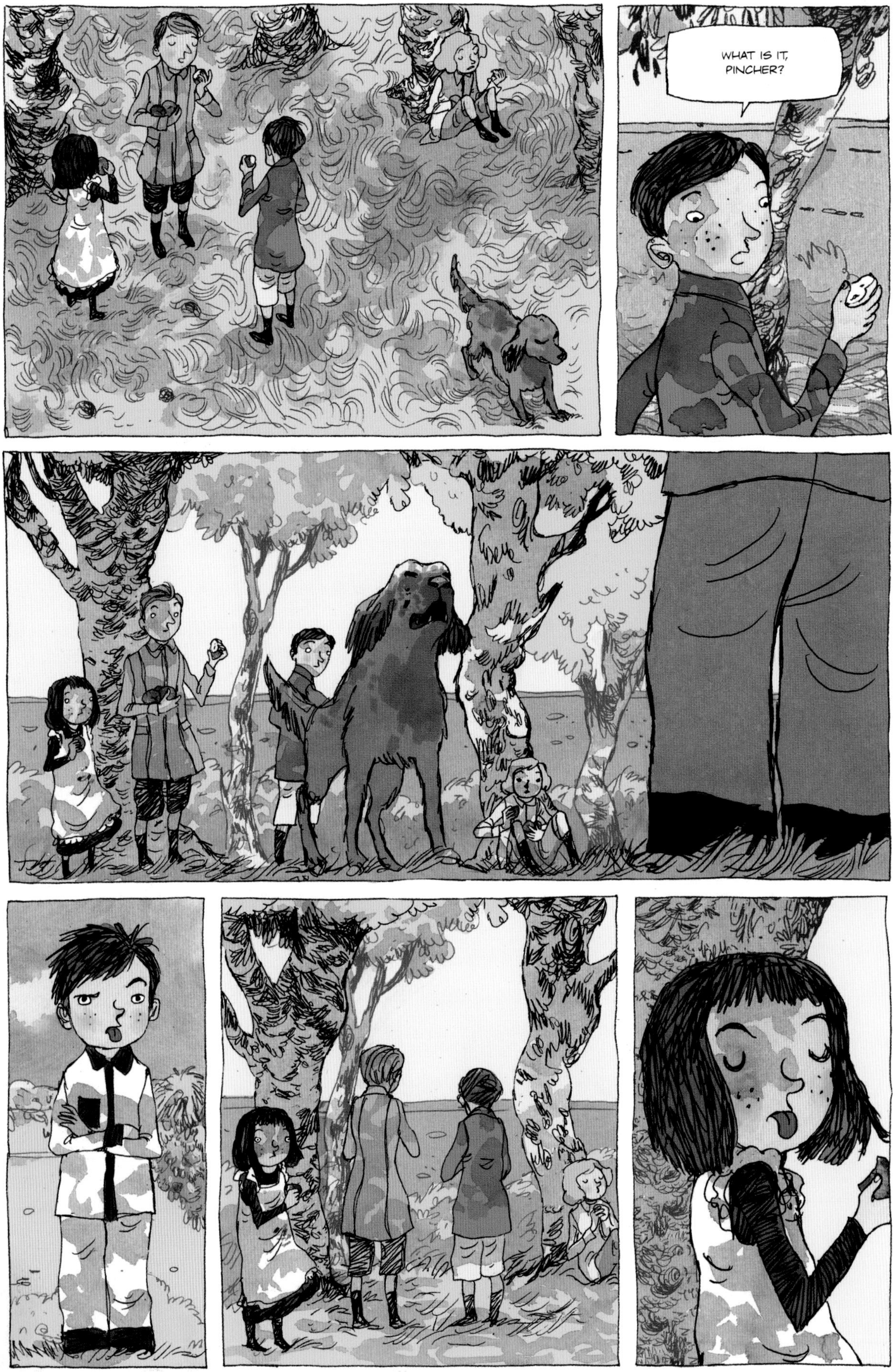
WHAT IS IT, PINCHER?

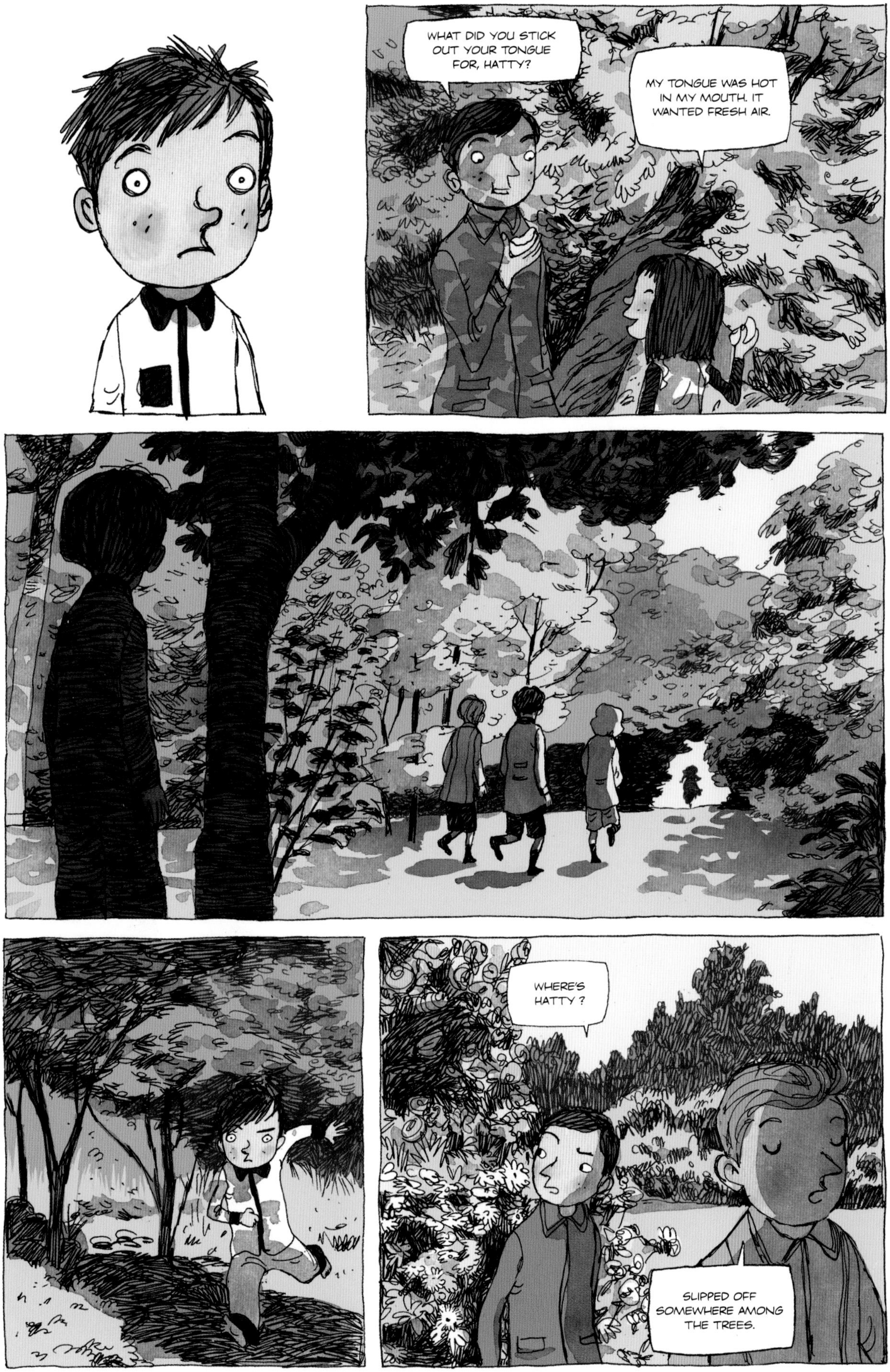

WHAT DID YOU STICK OUT YOUR TONGUE FOR, HATTY?
MY TONGUE WAS HOT IN MY MOUTH. IT WANTED FRESH AIR.
WHERE'S HATTY ?
SLIPPED OFF SOMEWHERE AMONG THE TREES.

COO-EEE !

I KNEW YOU WERE HIDING FROM ME AND WATCHING ME, JUST NOW.

JUST NOW!

WHY, I'VE HIDDEN AND WATCHED YOU, OFTEN AND OFTEN, BEFORE THIS! I SAW YOU WHEN YOU RAN ALONG BY THE NUT STUBS AND THEN USED MY SECRET HEDGE TUNNEL INTO THE MEADOW! I SAW YOU WHEN SUSAN WAS DUSTING AND YOU WAVED FROM THE TOP OF THE YEW TREE!

OH, I'VE SEEN YOU OFTEN — AND OFTEN — AND OFTEN — WHEN YOU NEVER KNEW IT!

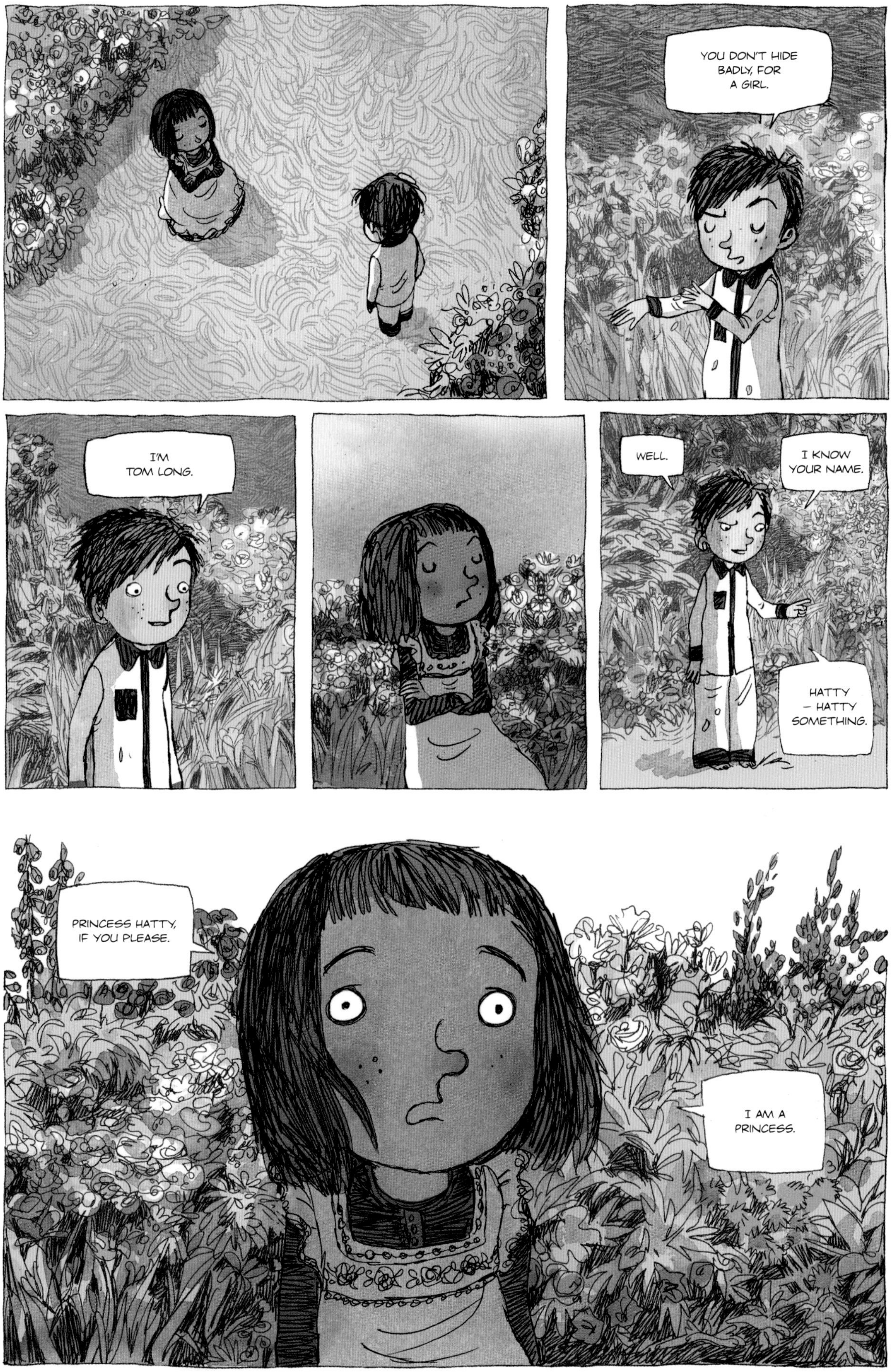

YOU DON'T HIDE BADLY, FOR A GIRL.
I'M TOM LONG.
WELL.
I KNOW YOUR NAME.
HATTY – HATTY SOMETHING.
PRINCESS HATTY, IF YOU PLEASE.
I AM A PRINCESS.

YOU CAN KISS MY HAND.

HATTY CAN SEE ME AND HEAR ME!

I WILL PERMIT YOU TO CALL ME PRINCESS.

AND NOW, I WILL ALLOW MYSELF TO PLAY WITH YOU.

I AM HELD HERE A PRISONER. I AM A PRINCESS IN DISGUISE. THERE IS SOMEONE HERE WHO CALLS HERSELF MY AUNT, BUT SHE ISN'T SO: SHE IS WICKED AND CRUEL TO ME. AND THOSE AREN'T MY COUSINS, EITHER, ALTHOUGH I HAVE TO CALL THEM SO. NOW YOU KNOW MY WHOLE SECRET.

SHE SHOWED ME NEW HIDING PLACES IN THE GARDEN.

YOU HAVE TO LISTEN INTENTLY AND MOVE EXACTLY — AND NOISELESSLY, OF COURSE — SO THAT THE TRUNK IS ALWAYS BETWEEN YOURSELF AND THE SEARCHER.

DID YOU ONCE LEAVE A WRITTEN MESSAGE HERE?

DID YOU ONCE FIND ONE?

YES — A LETTER TO FAIRIES.

FAIRIES!

WHOEVER COULD HAVE PUT IT THERE?

TO FAIRIES! JUST FANCY!

COME ON, TOM! I'LL SHOW YOU MORE!

LOOK, IT'S SENSITIVE. IF I TOUCH IT WITH MY FINGER . . .

COME ON, LET'S LOOK THROUGH THE COLORED GLASS ON THE DOOR!

AND IF YOU LOOK THROUGH THE STAR . . .

YOU CAN'T SEE ANYTHING.

SOMETIMES I LIKE THAT THE BEST OF ALL. YOU LOOK AND SEE NOTHING, AND YOU MIGHT THINK THERE WASN'T A GARDEN AT ALL; BUT, ALL THE TIME, OF COURSE, THERE IS, WAITING FOR YOU.

I HAVE SO MANY QUESTIONS FOR HATTY, BUT WHEN I AM IN THE GARDEN, I FORGET.

THIS ONE IS CALLED "THE MATTERHORN,"

WHERE DOES THE GARDEN COME FROM? WHAT DOES IT ALL MEAN?

THIS ONE IS "THE LOOK-OUT,"

AND THIS ONE, "THE STEPS OF ST. PAUL'S."

AND HERE . . .

. . . IS "TRICKSY."

WHAT ARE YOU UP TO THERE, HATTY? FOR THE LAST FIVE MINUTES YOU'VE BEEN TALKING AND NODDING AND SMILING AND LISTENING, ALL BY YOURSELF.

I AM NOT BY MYSELF. I AM TALKING TO A FRIEND OF MINE.

WHERE IS HE?

NEXT TO ME . . .

HA! HA! HA!

HA! HA! REALLY, COUSIN HATTY, PEOPLE WILL THINK YOU'VE LOST YOUR SENSES!

AND NOW HE'LL GO AND TELL THE OTHERS, AND THEY'LL JEER AT ME, AND AUNT GRACE WILL SAY IT SHOWS HOW UNFIT I AM TO GO ANYWHERE WITH OTHER CHILDREN, OUTSIDE, IN THE VILLAGE.

WELL, THEN, WHY DID YOU TELL EDGAR ABOUT ME?

ONE MUST TELL THE TRUTH, MUSTN'T ONE?

HUBERT AND JAMES AND EDGAR USED TO PLAY AT FOREST OUTLAWS, WITH BOWS AND ARROWS THEY MADE THEMSELVES.

NOT ME, THOUGH.

I TAUGHT HATTY HOW TO MAKE A BOW. SHE WENT TO GET A KITCHEN KNIFE.

WHY DIDN'T YOU?

I HAD TO TELL HER HOW TO USE IT. SHE WAS CLUMSY WITH IT AT FIRST.

THEY SAID I WAS TOO YOUNG; AND, THEN, WHEN I WAS OLD ENOUGH, THEY SAID THEY WERE TOO OLD.

I COULDN'T HELP HER BEND THE BOW, AS I COULDN'T TOUCH THINGS.

IN THE END SHE WENT TO ABEL, THE GARDENER.

YOU DID THIS, MISS HATTY?

YES, INDEED I DID.

AYE, BUT WHO TAUGHT YOU?

SOMEONE.

WELL, WHOEVER IT WAS TAUGHT YOU, TAKE CARE HE DON'T TEACH YOU TROUBLE WITH IT.

TROUBLE?

TROUBLE FOR YOURSELF, MISS HATTY.

HATTY SHOT HER ARROWS UP INTO THE AIR AT RANDOM.

AND ONE BROKE A WINDOW.

THANK YOU. AUNT WON'T EVEN KNOW.

NO.

BUT DO YOU REMEMBER WHAT I TOLD YOU OF.

THE NEXT TROUBLE WE GOT INTO . . .

I'VE FOUND IT!

. . . ABEL COULDN'T SAVE US FROM.

47

PETER, YOU SHOULD HAVE SEEN IT! WHEN I GOT BACK TO THE GARDEN, THE GEESE HAD TRAMPLED EVERYTHING.

BUT THE WORST THING WAS THAT WHEN ABEL AND THE COUSINS TRIED TO DRIVE THEM BACK INTO THE MEADOW . . .

PINCHER TURNED UP.

I DIDN'T KNOW THAT ANGRY GEESE COULD BE SO TERRIFYING.

AND AS FOR THE DAMAGE — THE FLOWER BEDS, THE LAWN . . .

ABEL! HOW DID THEY GET IN THE GARDEN?

HOW THEY MADE THAT WAY UNBEKNOWNST IS MORE THAN I KNOW!

UNLESS THE DEVIL HIMSELF TAUGHT THEM!

THEY DIDN'T MAKE IT.

HATTY DID.

HARRIET!

YOU ARE TO BLAME.

YOU THANKLESS PAUPER. I RECEIVED YOU INTO MY HOME AS A DUTY TO MY LATE HUSBAND, YOUR UNCLE.

I EXPECTED YOU TO BE GRATEFUL, DUTIFUL, AND OBEDIENT.

INSTEAD, YOU ARE NOTHING BUT AN EXPENSE AND A SHAME TO ME AND TO YOUR COUSINS.

LIAR!

CRIMINAL!

MONSTER !

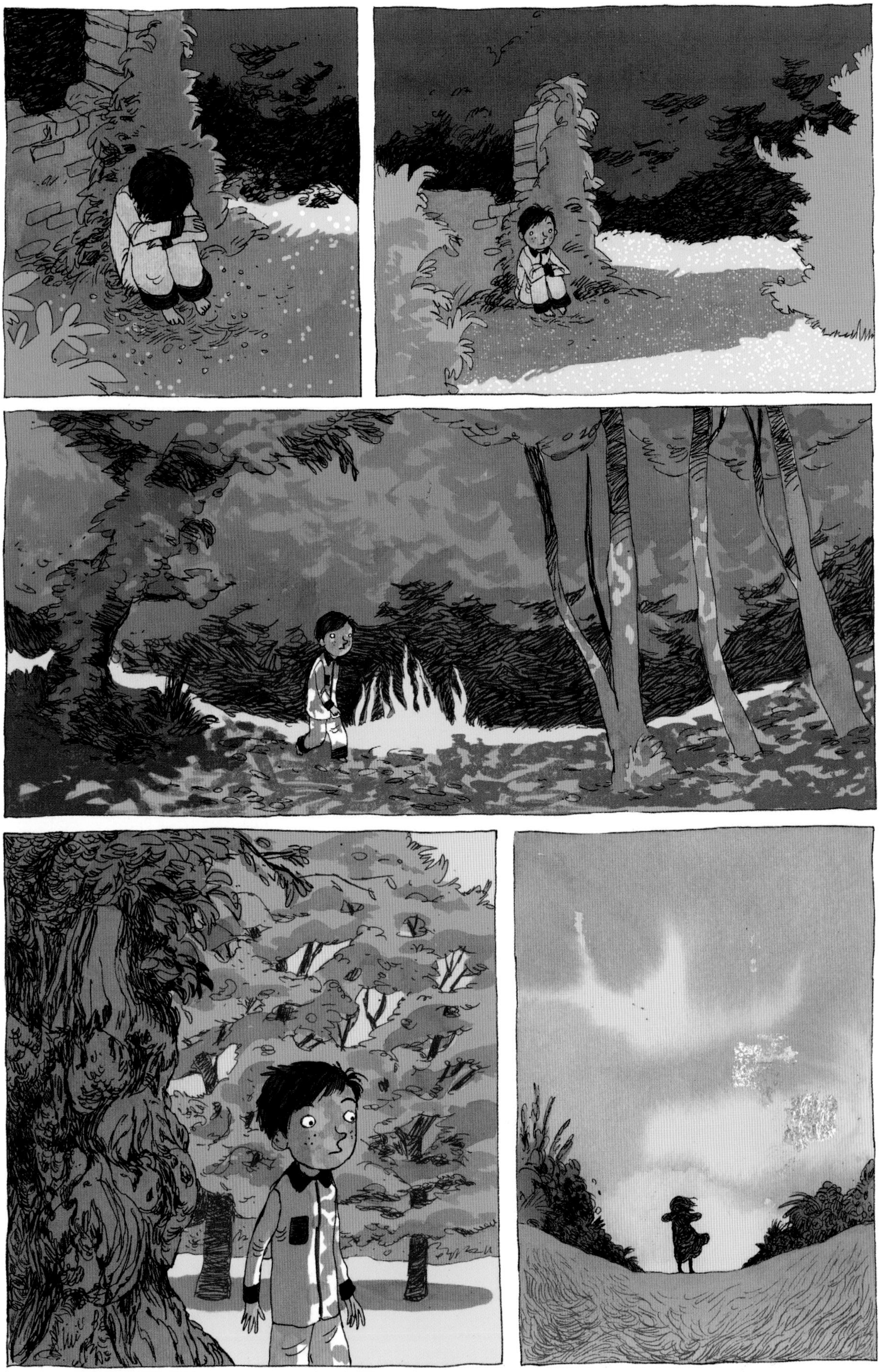

DON'T CRY.

I WANT TO GO HOME. I WANT MY FATHER! I WANT MY MOTHER!

OH, COUSIN!

PETER, IT WAS HATTY, BUT MUCH YOUNGER.

SHE HAD MISTAKEN ME FOR ONE OF HER COUSINS.

I WISH I HADN'T TO GO HOME TOMORROW.

WHAT?

I WISH I HADN'T TO GO HOME TOMORROW.

WOUD YOU LIKE TO STAY?

YES.

WE'LL SEND A TELEGRAM AT ONCE.

WHY DO YOU WANT TO STAY HERE?

I WON'T, IF YOU'D RATHER NOT.

NO . . . NO . . . BUT I WONDERED WHY . . .

WHAT IS THERE TO INTEREST A BOY HERE — TO PASS HIS TIME EVEN?

I JUST LIKE IT HERE.

AS I AM OUT OF QUARANTINE NOW, A.G. FEELS OBLIGED TO ORGANIZE EXCURSIONS SO I AM NOT COOPED UP INDOORS ANYMORE.

I HAVE BEEN TO MUSEUMS, TO SHOPS, AND TODAY TO THE CINEMA.

TOM, YOU'VE BEEN STANDING IN THAT PUDDLE ALL THIS TIME!

I HOPE YOU DON'T CATCH COLD.

I'M GOING TO WRITE TO MY SISTER TO TELL HER YOU WON'T BE FIT TO TRAVEL FOR SOME TIME YET.

PETER, IT'S A WONDERFUL PIECE OF LUCK — THE NEXT BEST THING TO MEASLES.

AND WHEN I'M IN THE GARDEN, THE FEVERISHNESS LEAVES ME.

HATTY MUST HAVE LIVED HERE, LONG, LONG AGO — HERE SHE LIVED, HERE DIED . . .

I AM SURE MRS. BARTHOLOMEW MUST KNOW SOMETHING, BECAUSE OF THE CLOCK.

PERHAPS HER FAMILY HAVE OWNED THIS HOUSE FOR GENERATIONS.

I MUST GO TO SEE HER.

MRS. BARTHOLOMEW DOESN'T LIKE CHILDREN!

BUT WITH ME, IT WILL BE DIFFERENT . . .

IT'S SO NICE OF YOU TO COME AND SEE ME.

SHE WILL OFFER ME TEA AND CAKE.

A LITTLE GIRL CALLED HARRIET, OR HATTY?

WHY, YES, MY LATE HUSBAND TOLD ME ONCE OF SUCH A CHILD — OH! LONG AGO! AN ONLY CHILD SHE WAS, AND AN ORPHAN. WHEN HER PARENTS DIED, HER AUNT TOOK HER INTO THIS HOUSE TO LIVE. HER AUNT WAS A DISAGREEABLE WOMAN . . .

SHE WILL TELL ME THE WHOLE STORY.

AND SINCE THEN, TOM, THEY SAY THAT SHE HAUNTS THIS HOUSE. THEY SAY THAT THOSE WHO ARE LUCKY MAY GO DOWN, ABOUT WHEN THE CLOCK STRIKES FOR MIDNIGHT, AND OPEN WHAT WAS ONCE THE GARDEN DOOR AND SEE THE GHOST OF THAT GARDEN AND OF THE LITTLE GIRL.

WHEN MR. BARTHOLOMEW LIVED IN THIS HOUSE —

BUT I DON'T THINK MR. BARTHOLOMEW EVER DID LIVE HERE. DO YOU, ALAN?

BUT, AUNT GWEN, THIS WAS HIS FAMILY HOME.

MR. BARTHOLOMEW, WHOEVER HE WAS, NEVER LIVED IN THIS HOUSE. MRS. BARTHOLOMEW WAS A WIDOW WHEN SHE CAME HERE; AND THAT WASN'T SO MANY YEARS AGO, EITHER.

BUT WHAT ABOUT THE CLOCK?

WHAT CLOCK?

THE GRANDFATHER CLOCK IN THE HALL. YOU SAID IT BELONGED TO MRS. BARTHOLOMEW; BUT THAT CLOCK HAS ALWAYS BEEN IN THIS HOUSE. IT WAS HERE LONG, LONG AGO — IT WAS HERE WHEN THE HOUSE HAD A GARDEN.

NOW, WHAT REASON HAVE YOU FOR SUPPOSING ALL THIS, TOM?

...

YOU KNOW, ALAN, THE CLOCK CERTAINLY MUST HAVE BEEN HERE A LONG TIME, BECAUSE OF ITS SCREWS AT THE BACK HAVING RUSTED INTO THE WALL.

WELL, NOW, TOM, THAT MIGHT EXPLAIN A LITTLE. THE CLOCK MAY WELL HAVE BEEN HERE A LONG TIME, AS YOU SAY, AND DURING THAT TIME THE SCREWS RUSTED UP. AFTER THAT HAPPENED, THE CLOCK COULDN'T BE MOVED WITHOUT DANGER OF DAMAGING IT. WHEN OLD MRS. BARTHOLOMEW CAME, SHE HAD TO BUY THE CLOCK WITH THE HOUSE. YOU SEE, TOM? IT'S ALL QUITE STRAIGHTFORWARD, IF YOU REASON IT OUT.

WHAT'S IT LIKE — I MEAN, I WONDER WHAT IT'S LIKE TO BE DEAD AND A GHOST?

WHAT IS IT LIKE TO BE A GHOST?

LIKE?

AH, TELL ME, TOM!

I'M NOT A GHOST!

DON'T BE SILLY, TOM. YOU FORGET THAT I SAW YOU GO RIGHT THROUGH THE ORCHARD DOOR WHEN IT WAS SHUT.

THAT PROVES WHAT I SAY! I'M NOT A GHOST, BUT THE ORCHARD DOOR IS, AND THAT WAS WHY I COULD GO THROUGH IT. THE DOOR'S A GHOST, AND THE GARDEN'S A GHOST; AND SO ARE YOU, TOO!

INDEED I'M NOT; YOU ARE! AND YOU MAKE A SILLY LITTLE GHOST! WHY DO YOU THINK YOU WEAR THOSE CLOTHES OF YOURS? NONE OF MY COUSINS EVER PLAYED IN THE GARDEN IN CLOTHES LIKE THAT. SUCH OUTDOOR CLOTHES CAN'T BELONG TO NOWADAYS, I KNOW! SUCH CLOTHES!

THEY'RE MY PAJAMAS. MY BEST VISITING PAJAMAS! I SLEEP IN THEM.

AND YOU GO ABOUT SO, IN THE DAYTIME, ALWAYS IN YOUR NIGHT-CLOTHES!

YOU WEAR STRANGE CLOTHES THAT NO ONE WEARS NOWADAYS, BECAUSE YOU'RE A GHOST. WHY, I'M THE ONLY PERSON IN THE GARDEN WHO SEES YOU! I CAN SEE A GHOST.

DO YOU HEAR ME? **YOU'RE** A GHOST! YOU'RE DEAD AND GONE AND A GHOST!

I'M NOT DEAD — OH, PLEASE, TOM!

I'M NOT DEAD!

AND I'M NOT A GHOST EITHER!

I THINK I KNOW WHEN HATTY LIVED. I LOOKED IN A BOOK CALLED *INQUIRE WITHIN UPON EVERYTHING*, WHICH A.G. KEEPS IN THE KITCHEN.

JUDGING BY THE CLOTHES HATTY AND HER COUSINS WEAR, IT WAS THE REIGN OF QUEEN VICTORIA. THAT'S OVER A HUNDRED YEARS AGO . . .

WOULD WOMEN HAVE BEEN WEARING LONG SKIRTS AT, SAY, THE BEGINNING OF QUEEN VICTORIA'S REIGN?

OH, YES; ALL DURING VICTORIA'S REIGN, AND AFTER.

HATTY! WHY DIDN'T YOU ANSWER? DIDN'T YOU HEAR ME? I CALLED AND CALLED AND CALLED.

I WAS HELPING ABEL. YOU WON'T LIKE IT. HE BURNED THE BOW AND ARROWS.

HE MADE ME PROMISE NOT TO USE THE KITCHEN KNIVES AGAIN, AND HE SAID HE'D GIVE ME A LITTLE KNIFE ALL OF MY OWN.

WHAT KIND OF KNIFE?

HE BOUGHT IT AT THE FAIR, TO GIVE TO SUSAN; BUT SHE WOULDN'T HAVE IT FROM HIM, BECAUSE IT'S UNLUCKY TO HAVE A KNIFE FROM YOUR SWEETHEART. SO ABEL GAVE IT TO ME.

WELL! YOU CERTAINLY COULDN'T CUT YOURSELF WITH THAT! YOU COULD JUST ABOUT CUT BUTTER WITH IT, THAT'S ALL!

I'VE CUT MORE THAN BUTTER WITH IT, ALREADY. COME, AND I'LL SHOW YOU.

THIS MEANS: HATTY MELBOURNE HAS CLIMBED THIS TREE.

WITH MY KNIFE, I'VE CARVED MY INITIALS ON ALL THE YEW TREES.

EXCEPT FOR TRICKSY, OF COURSE.

ONE DAY I'LL CLIMB TRICKSY.

I TAUGHT HATTY HOW TO **SWARM** TRICKSY.

I MUSTN'T GET MY CLOTHES DIRTY OR MY AUNT WILL PUNISH ME.

HATTY COULD ALWAYS FIND SOMETHING NEW TO DO IN THE GARDEN.

JAMES ONCE WALKED ALONG THE TOP OF THE WALL.

WELL, I'M NOT GOING TO. THAT WALL'S FAR TOO HIGH, AND IT'LL BE VERY NARROW ALONG THE TOP.

OH, TOM, I DIDN'T MEAN THAT YOU SHOULD WALK IT! JAMES ONLY DID IT FOR A DARE. COUSIN EDGAR DARED HIM, AND JAMES DID IT. HE WALKED THE WHOLE LENGTH, AND THEN HE CLIMBED DOWN, AND THEN HE FOUGHT COUSIN EDGAR, AND THEN HE WAS SICK. AND COUSIN HUBERT HEARD ABOUT IT ALL AFTERWARDS AND WAS VERY ANGRY, BECAUSE HE SAID JAMES MIGHT HAVE FALLEN AND BROKEN HIS NECK.

WELL I'M SURE I COULD DO IT TOO.

OH, TOM!

DON'T WORRY. IT'S ALL RIGHT FOR ME.

WHAT DO YOU SEE, TOM?

COME BACK AND COME DOWN NOW, TOM!

WHAT IS THERE BEYOND THE GARDEN?

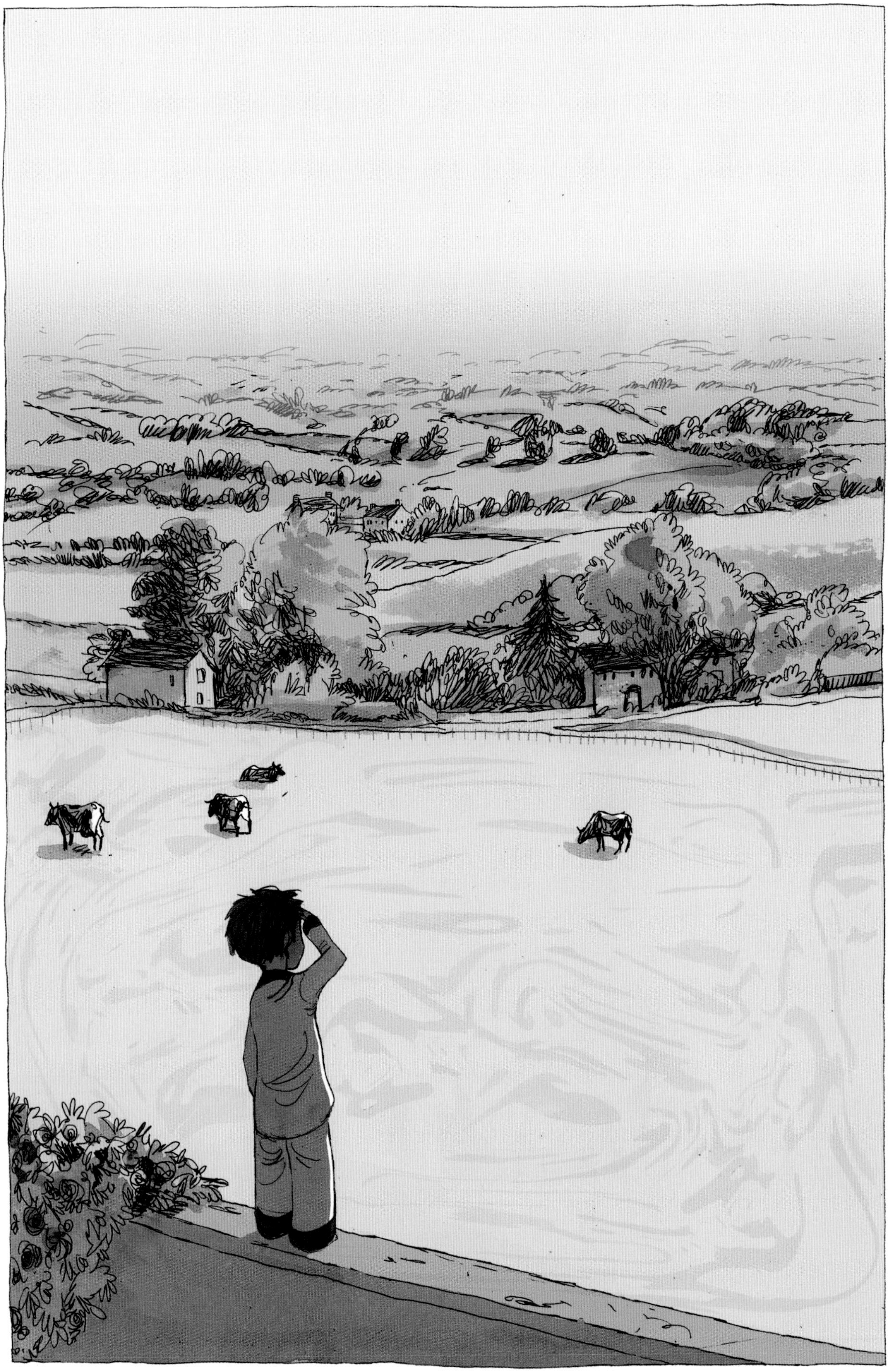

WHAT ON EARTH WAS THE MATTER?

ABEL THOUGHT I WAS GOING TO WALK ALONG THE TOP OF THE WALL, AS JAMES DID. HE WANTED TO STOP ME BECAUSE OF THE DANGER.

I THOUGHT HE WAS GOING TO BEAT YOU.

HE MADE ME KNEEL DOWN ON THE PATH AND SWEAR ON HIS BIBLE — SWEAR NEVER TO CLIMB THE WALL AND WALK ALONG IT.

WAS HE VERY ANGRY?

NO. I THINK — SOMEHOW — HE WAS FRIGHTENED.

FRIGHTENED? YOU MEAN THAT **YOU** WERE FRIGHTENED; **HE** WAS ANGRY.

WHY DID HE SUDDENLY THINK YOU MIGHT TRY TO CLIMB THE WALL?

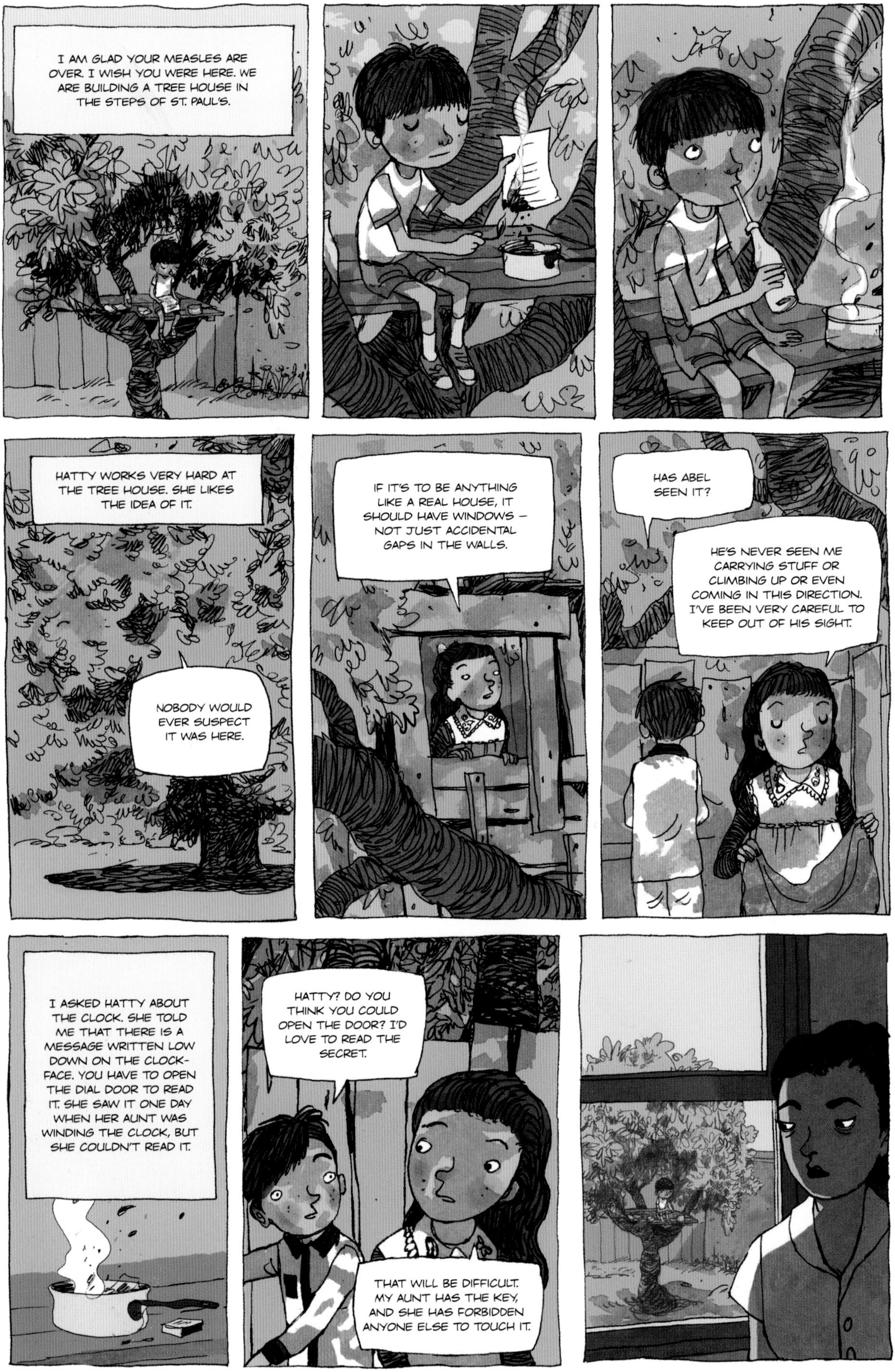
I AM GLAD YOUR MEASLES ARE OVER. I WISH YOU WERE HERE. WE ARE BUILDING A TREE HOUSE IN THE STEPS OF ST. PAUL'S.
HATTY WORKS VERY HARD AT THE TREE HOUSE. SHE LIKES THE IDEA OF IT.
NOBODY WOULD EVER SUSPECT IT WAS HERE.
IF IT'S TO BE ANYTHING LIKE A REAL HOUSE, IT SHOULD HAVE WINDOWS – NOT JUST ACCIDENTAL GAPS IN THE WALLS.
HAS ABEL SEEN IT?
HE'S NEVER SEEN ME CARRYING STUFF OR CLIMBING UP OR EVEN COMING IN THIS DIRECTION. I'VE BEEN VERY CAREFUL TO KEEP OUT OF HIS SIGHT.
I ASKED HATTY ABOUT THE CLOCK. SHE TOLD ME THAT THERE IS A MESSAGE WRITTEN LOW DOWN ON THE CLOCK-FACE. YOU HAVE TO OPEN THE DIAL DOOR TO READ IT. SHE SAW IT ONE DAY WHEN HER AUNT WAS WINDING THE CLOCK, BUT SHE COULDN'T READ IT.
HATTY? DO YOU THINK YOU COULD OPEN THE DOOR? I'D LOVE TO READ THE SECRET.
THAT WILL BE DIFFICULT. MY AUNT HAS THE KEY, AND SHE HAS FORBIDDEN ANYONE ELSE TO TOUCH IT.

THERE ARE NO OTHER CHILDREN THERE AND TOM NEVER SEEMS TO GO ANYWHERE VERY SPECIAL.

DOES HE TELL YOU MORE, PETER, IN HIS LETTERS TO YOU? THEY SEEM LONG ENOUGH.

I THINK HE JUST LIKES STAYING IN THAT APARTMENT.

I SUPPOSE HE'LL HAVE TO COME HOME FOR SCHOOL, ANYWAY.

FOR SCHOOL? WHY, WE MUST HAVE HIM HOME BEFORE THAT, PETER!

YOU SURELY DON'T WANT TO SPEND ALL THIS SUMMER WITHOUT TOM?

I SUPPOSE—

I SUPPOSE THAT, IF TOM DOESN'T WANT TO COME AWAY FROM AUNT GWEN'S YET, I COULDN'T GO THERE TOO, AND STAY THERE WITH HIM?

YOU SURELY MEAN THAT YOU'D LIKE TO BE **HERE** WITH TOM. YOU WANT HIM TO COME HOME.

YOU CAN'T REALLY WANT TO GO AND STAY WITH HIM IN THAT APARTMENT.

I DO!

I WANT TO GO!

TOM, THERE'S A CRACKED BOUGH THIS SIDE — IS IT ALL RIGHT? HAVE YOU EVER SAT ON IT?

A CRACKED BOUGH? OH, YES, I'VE BEEN OUT ON THAT ONE.

ONLY I DARESAY I'M DIFFERENT: I WOULDN'T ADVISE YOU —

OH!

CRAAAAAAACKK

EEEEHAAAAAAAAA

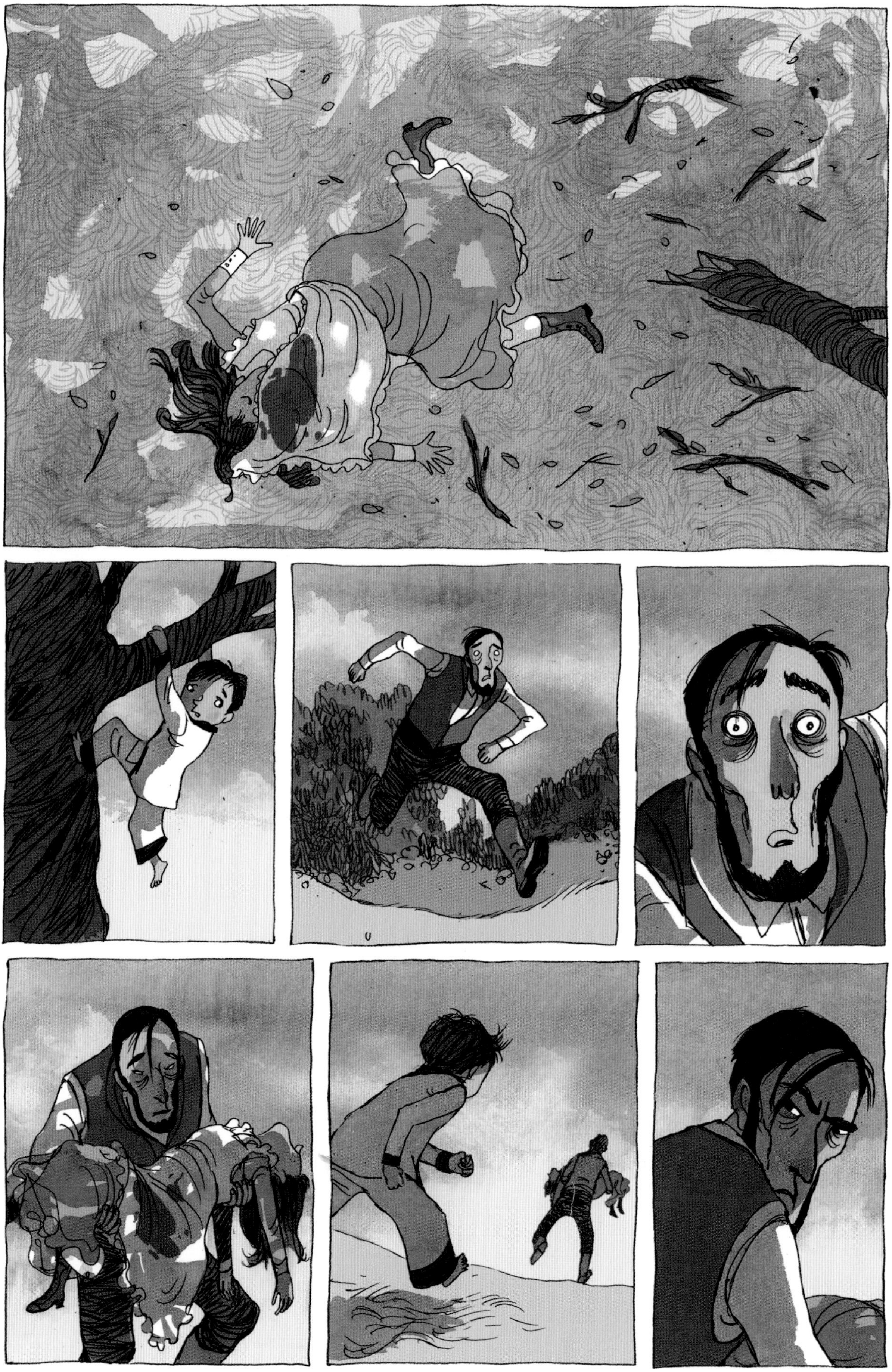

GET YOU GONE!

GET YOU BACK TO HELL, WHERE YOU COME FROM! I KNOW YOU. I'VE SEEN YOU ALWAYS, AND THOUGHT BEST NOT TO SEE YOU; AND HEARD YOU AND THOUGHT BEST TO SEEM DEAF; BUT I'VE KNOWN YOU, AND KNOWN YOU FOR WHAT YOU ARE!

MAY THE LORD KEEP ME FROM ALL THE WORKS OF THE DEVIL, THAT HE HURT ME NOT.

ABEL, PLEASE, HOW IS HATTY?'

ABEL — ABEL — ABEL, SHE'S NOT DEAD, IS SHE? SHE'S NOT DEAD?

NO.

SHE'S ALIVE.

I WENT BACK INTO THE HOUSE . . .

. . . BUT THINGS WERE DIFFERENT FROM USUAL.

THIS TIME, THE FURNITURE DID NOT DISSOLVE IN FRONT OF ME. I WENT UPSTAIRS AND I WAS STILL IN THE MELBOURNES' HOUSE.

I THOUGHT I COULD FIND HATTY'S ROOM AND SEE HOW SHE WAS. ABEL HAD SAID: "SHE'S ALIVE;" BUT PERHAPS THAT MEANT, "SHE'S JUST ALIVE," OR EVEN, "SHE'S ALIVE, BUT CAN'T LIVE LONG."

I WONDERED IF A GHOST COULD DIE.

MOTHER?

WHO IS THAT?

JAMES.

YOU CAN COME IN.

PETER, I DIDN'T UNDERSTAND. JAMES . . . WAS A MAN! I MEAN AN ADULT MAN . . .

HOW IS HATTY?

HATTY WILL DO WELL ENOUGH.

BUT WHAT WAS SHE DOING, TO HAVE THE ACCIDENT? CLIMBING TREES, IF YOU PLEASE!

HAS SHE NO SENSE OF WHAT IS FITTING TO HER SEX AND TO HER AGE NOW?

HATTY IS YOUNG FOR HER AGE. PERHAPS IT COMES FROM HER BEING BY HERSELF SO MUCH — PLAYING ALONE — ALWAYS IN THE GARDEN.

OH, YOU WERE ALWAYS KIND TO HER! AND SO SHE IS NEVER TO GROW UP! WHAT IS TO HAPPEN TO HER, IF SO?

OF COURSE HATTY WILL GROW UP.

WE COULD MAKE HER WANT MORE. I'LL TELL HER THAT WHEN SHE IS QUITE WELL AGAIN, WE ALL WANT HER TO GO OUT, TO MAKE FRIENDS.

SHE DOESN'T WANT TO. SHE WANTS ONLY HER GARDEN.

YOU WILL WASTE YOUR PITY AND YOUR BREATH WITH HARRIET. YOU CAN SAY WHAT YOU LIKE TO HER; YOU CAN DO WHAT YOU LIKE WITH HER; AND THE LESS I SEE OF HER, THE BETTER.

I AM GOING TO SEE HER NOW.

I WAITED OUTSIDE HATTY'S ROOM UNTIL JAMES CAME OUT, TO GO AND SEE HER MYSELF.

TOM . . .

WELL, HOW ARE YOU?

JAMES SAYS I MUST DO OTHER THINGS BESIDES FALLING OUT OF TREES, IN THE FUTURE.

THINGS WITHOUT ME?

OH, NO, TOM.

WHENEVER YOU WANT TO COME, SO YOU SHALL!

YOU HAVE A NICE BEDROOM.

YOU'VE BARS ACROSS YOUR WINDOWS.

IT WAS MY COUSINS' NURSERY, WHEN THEY WERE LITTLE.

AFTER THAT . . . IT BECAME MY BEDROOM.

I LIKE YOUR ROOM BETTER, AND I LIKE YOUR VIEW MUCH BETTER.

BETTER THAN WHAT, TOM?

BETTER — BETTER THAN IF THERE WERE NOTHING BUT HOUSES OPPOSITE.

DON'T BE SILLY, TOM!

THEN WE'D BE LIVING IN A TOWN!

I'M GOING TO SHOW YOU SOMETHING.

OPEN THE CUPBOARD — THE BOTTOM DOOR.

LOOK AT THE BACK. THE LAST FLOORBOARD ON THE RIGHT. LEVER IT UP. IT'S MY SECRET SPACE. I'M GOING TO SHOW YOU MY HOARD.

THE PHOTO IS MY MOTHER AND FATHER, LONG AGO. YOU REMEMBER, TOM, I ONCE USED TO PRETEND TO YOU THAT THEY WERE A KING AND QUEEN.

I'M SO TIRED . . .

I SHALL SEE YOU TOMORROW.

YOU ALWAYS SAY THAT . . .

AND THEN IT'S OFTEN MONTHS AND MONTHS BEFORE YOU COME AGAIN.

I COME EVERY NIGHT!

I THOUGHT I WOULD HAVE TO GO BACK OUT INTO THE GARDEN AND IN AGAIN FOR THINGS TO GO BACK TO NORMAL.

BUT . . .?

I . . .

I SHALL NEVER GET BACK!

I'LL TELL HATTY. I'LL ASK HER WHAT TO DO. I'LL TELL HER EVERYTHING, EVEN IF IT DOES MEAN TALKING ABOUT GHOSTS.

WHEN I WENT BACK INTO HER BEDROOM, HATTY WAS SLEEPING. I DIDN'T WANT TO WAKE HER. I LAY DOWN BESIDE HER BED AND WAITED FOR HER TO WAKE UP.

I WOKE UP IN MY OWN ROOM! IT WAS VERY EARLY. I WENT TO CLOSE THE FRONT DOOR OF THE FLAT.

IT'S TIME TO GET UP, TOM. THE POST HAS JUST BROUGHT A LETTER FROM HOME — ONE FOR YOU FROM PETER, AND ONE FOR ME FROM YOUR MOTHER.

DEAR TOM, **BEWARE!** MOTHER IS WRITING TO AUNT GWEN TO SAY CAN YOU COME HOME AT THE END OF THE WEEK AND THIS TIME YOU REALLY ARE TO. I THINK MOTHER WILL SAY YOU MUST COME BECAUSE I MISS YOU SO MUCH BUT I DON'T WANT YOU TO COME AWAY. I LIKE ALL YOU WRITE IN YOUR LETTERS. TELL ME SOME MORE. I WISH I WERE THERE BUT MOTHER AND FATHER SAY NO. I WISH WE HAD MORE TREES AND A RIVER NEAR AND A HIGH WALL. I **WISH** I WERE THERE.

WELL, TOM, SO WE MUST REALLY SAY GOOD-BYE TO YOU SOON.

WHEN?

ON SATURDAY. THERE'S A CHEAP TRAIN ON SATURDAY MORNING.

YOUR MOTHER SAYS THAT PETER HAS BEEN MISSING YOU VERY MUCH. WE COULD HARDLY EXPECT TO KEEP YOU LONGER WITH US HERE — UNLESS WE ADOPTED YOU.

IF YOU ADOPTED ME . . .

I WAS ONLY JOKING, TOM.

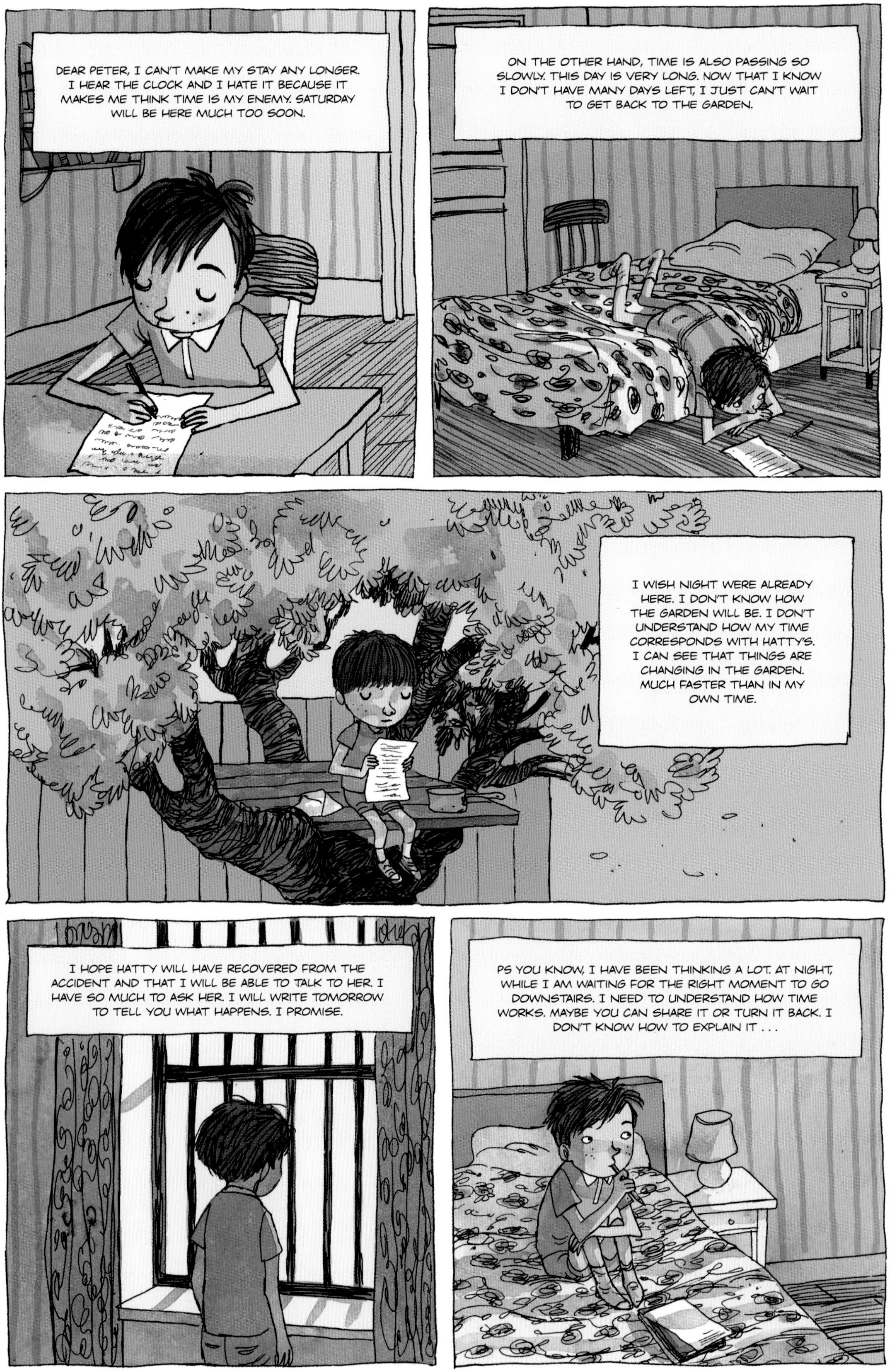
DEAR PETER, I CAN'T MAKE MY STAY ANY LONGER. I HEAR THE CLOCK AND I HATE IT BECAUSE IT MAKES ME THINK TIME IS MY ENEMY. SATURDAY WILL BE HERE MUCH TOO SOON.
ON THE OTHER HAND, TIME IS ALSO PASSING SO SLOWLY. THIS DAY IS VERY LONG. NOW THAT I KNOW I DON'T HAVE MANY DAYS LEFT, I JUST CAN'T WAIT TO GET BACK TO THE GARDEN.
I WISH NIGHT WERE ALREADY HERE. I DON'T KNOW HOW THE GARDEN WILL BE. I DON'T UNDERSTAND HOW MY TIME CORRESPONDS WITH HATTY'S. I CAN SEE THAT THINGS ARE CHANGING IN THE GARDEN. MUCH FASTER THAN IN MY OWN TIME.
I HOPE HATTY WILL HAVE RECOVERED FROM THE ACCIDENT AND THAT I WILL BE ABLE TO TALK TO HER. I HAVE SO MUCH TO ASK HER. I WILL WRITE TOMORROW TO TELL YOU WHAT HAPPENS. I PROMISE.
PS YOU KNOW, I HAVE BEEN THINKING A LOT. AT NIGHT, WHILE I AM WAITING FOR THE RIGHT MOMENT TO GO DOWNSTAIRS. I NEED TO UNDERSTAND HOW TIME WORKS. MAYBE YOU CAN SHARE IT OR TURN IT BACK. I DON'T KNOW HOW TO EXPLAIN IT . . .

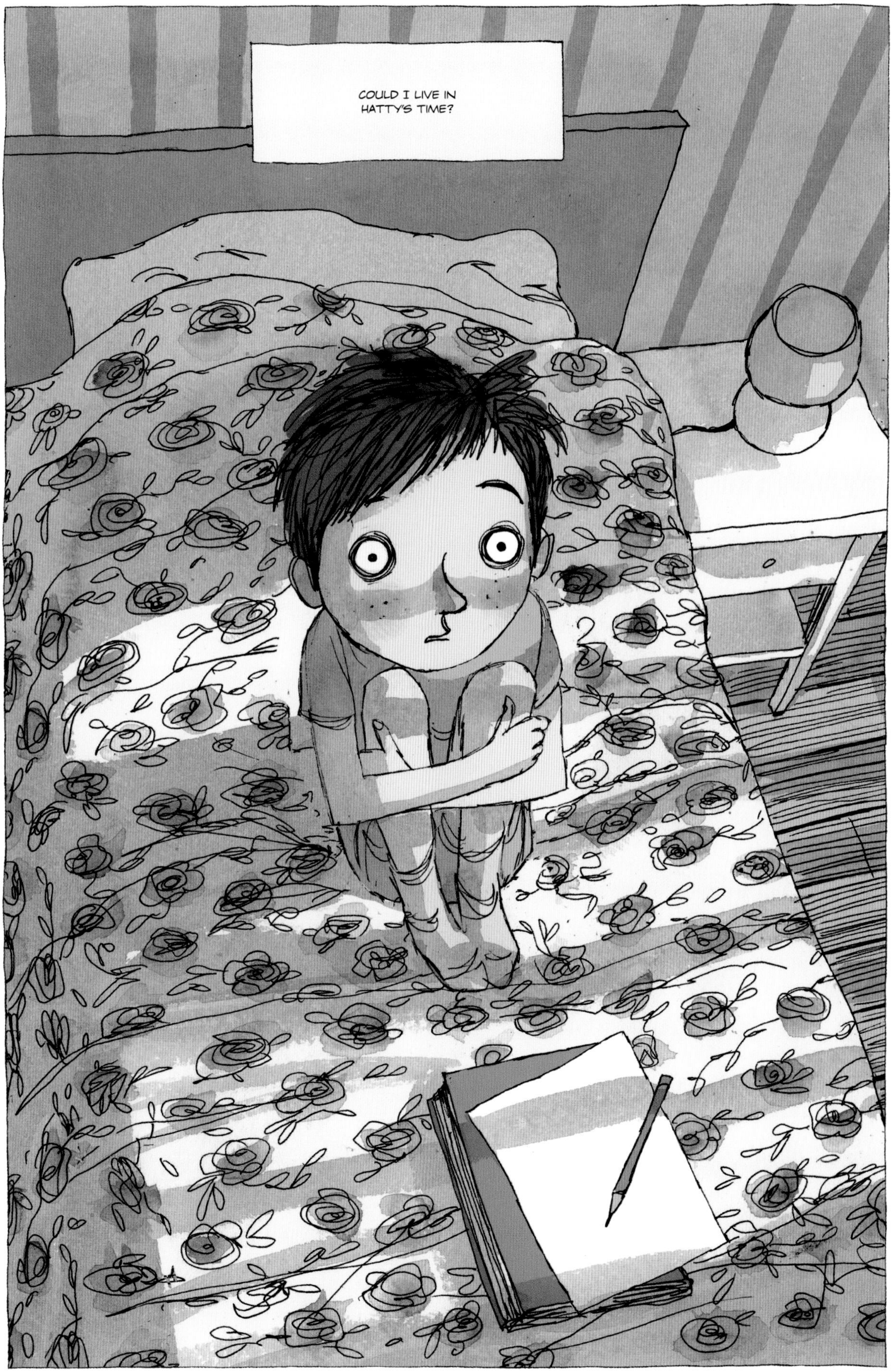
COULD I LIVE IN
HATTY'S TIME?

IT WAS THE FIRST TIME I'D SEEN SNOW IN THE GARDEN!

WHY, TOM! YOU'RE THINNER!

THINNER? NO, I'M FATTER.

I DIDN'T MEAN THAT; I MEANT THINNER **THROUGH**.

OH, NO, I DIDN'T MEAN THAT EITHER — AT LEAST, I DON'T KNOW WHAT I COULD HAVE MEANT, OR RATHER —

IT DOESN'T MATTER, BUT I WANT YOU TO FIND OUT FOR ME ABOUT THE PICTURE ON THE GRANDFATHER CLOCK. YOU DID SAY YOU WOULD.

DID I?

JUST BEFORE YOU FELL FROM OUR TREE HOUSE.

WHY, THAT WAS LONG AGO! IF YOU'VE WAITED SO LONG, TOM, COULDN'T YOU WAIT A LITTLE LONGER? WOULDN'T YOU RATHER WATCH ME SKATE?

YOU KNOW, I'VE REALLY IMPROVED. SOON I'LL BE ABLE TO GO SKATING WITH THE OTHERS.

THE OTHERS?

YES. JAMES, HUBERT AND EDGAR. BERTIE CODLING AND THE CHAPMAN GIRLS AND YOUNG BARTY AND ALL THE OTHERS.

PLEASE, HATTY! THE CLOCK!

VERY WELL. BUT QUICKLY. WE MUSTN'T LET MY AUNT SEE US.

SHE DOESN'T LET ANYONE TOUCH THE CLOCK.

BUT I KNOW WHERE THE KEY IS.

IT SAYS

TIME NO LONGER

TIME NO LONGER? NO LONGER THAN WHAT?

IT'S FROM THE BOOK OF REVELATION, IN THE BIBLE.

BUT WHAT DOES IT MEAN?

IT'S TO DO WITH AN ANGEL. NO ONE KNOWS FOR CERTAIN.

HUSH! DID YOU HEAR SOMEONE MOVING UPSTAIRS?

WHO HAS BEEN MEDDLING WITH THE TIME ON MY GRANDFATHER CLOCK?

WHAT IS TIME?

NEARLY SEVEN O'CLOCK.

I WANTED ANSWERS.

WHAT IS TIME – I MEAN, HOW DOES TIME WORK?

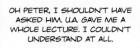

OH PETER, I SHOULDN'T HAVE ASKED HIM. U.A. GAVE ME A WHOLE LECTURE. I COULDN'T UNDERSTAND AT ALL.

I'VE HEARD A THEORY ABOUT AN ANGEL WHO SAID THAT, IN THE END, THERE WOULD BE TIME NO LONGER.

AN ANGEL!

WHAT ON EARTH HAVE ANGELS TO DO WITH SCIENTIFIC THEORIES?

U.A. WAS ANGRY. HE WENT FROM THE HOUSE SLAMMING THE DOOR BEHIND HIM, WITHOUT EVEN FINISHING HIS BREAKFAST. A.G. REPROACHED ME FOR CROSSING HIM.

THAT EVENING, U.A. APOLOGIZED AND TRIED TO EXPLAIN AGAIN. I STILL DIDN'T UNDERSTAND, BUT HE MUST HAVE SAID SOMETHING THAT SET ME THINKING IN A CERTAIN WAY.

EVERY NIGHT, I TRAVEL INTO THE PAST, A HUNDRED YEARS AND MORE. BUT I DO NOT ALWAYS GO BACK TO EXACTLY THE SAME TIME, EVERY NIGHT; NOR DO I TAKE TIME IN ITS USUAL ORDER. THE FIR TREE, FOR INSTANCE: I SAW IT STANDING, FALLEN AND THEN STANDING AGAIN. IN FLASHES, I HAVE SEEN HATTY'S TIME COVERING ABOUT TEN YEARS, WHILE MY OWN TIME ACHIEVED ONLY THE WEEKS OF A SUMMER HOLIDAY.

YOU MIGHT SAY THAT DIFFERENT PEOPLE HAVE DIFFERENT TIMES, ALTHOUGH OF COURSE, THEY'RE REALLY ALL BITS OF THE SAME BIG TIME.

WELL, ONE COULD SAY MORE ACCURATELY —

SO THAT I MIGHT BE ABLE, FOR SOME REASON, TO STEP BACK INTO SOMEONE ELSE'S TIME, IN THE PAST; OR, IF YOU LIKE . . .

THAT PERSON MIGHT STEP FORWARD INTO MY TIME, WHICH WOULD SEEM THE FUTURE TO HER, ALTHOUGH TO ME IT SEEMS THE PRESENT.

IT WOULD BE MUCH CLEARER, TOM, TO GO BACK TO THIS POINT "A" —

WHICHEVER WAY IT IS, SHE WOULD BE NO MORE A GHOST FROM THE PAST THAN I WOULD BE A GHOST FROM THE FUTURE.

WE'RE NEITHER OF US GHOSTS; AND THE GARDEN ISN'T EITHER. THAT SETTLES THAT.

WHAT ARE YOU TALKING ABOUT? GARDENS? AND WHAT SETTLES WHAT? WE'RE TALKING OF POSSIBILITIES — THEORIES.

BUT SUPPOSE SOMEONE REALLY HAD STEPPED OUT OF ONE TIME INTO ANOTHER — JUST LIKE THAT — THEN THAT WOULD BE PROOF.

PROOF!

I HAVE BEEN ABLE TO EXPLAIN TO YOU VERY LITTLE, TOM, IF I HAVE NOT EVEN CONVEYED TO YOU THAT PROOF — IN MATTERS OF TIME THEORY — PROOF . . . !

PETER, LAST NIGHT, BEFORE I WENT DOWN TO THE GARDEN, I HAD AN IDEA BUT IT NEEDED STILL TO BE WINTER...

OH, IT IS YOU, TOM!

I MISS YOU SOMETIMES, EVEN NOW — IN SPITE OF THE CHAPMAN GIRLS AND BARTY AND THE OTHERS — IN SPITE OF THE SKATING — OH, TOM, SKATING! I FEEL AS FREE AS A BIRD! I WANT TO GO FAR — SO FAR!

HATTY, WHERE DO YOU KEEP YOUR SKATES, WHEN YOU'RE NOT USING THEM, I MEAN?

IN THE BOOT CUPBOARD IN THE HALL.

WHY?

WILL YOU PROMISE ME SOMETHING?

WHAT?

WILL YOU PROMISE FIRST?

TELL ME, AND THEN I'LL PROMISE IF I POSSIBLY CAN.

WELL, I ONLY WANT YOU TO KEEP YOUR SKATES NOW IN THAT SECRET PLACE YOU SHOWED ME. IN YOUR BEDROOM CUPBOARD, UNDER THE FLOORBOARDS. AND IF YOU EVER GO AWAY, PROMISE TO LEAVE THEM THERE.

GO AWAY? BUT...

BUT MY SKATES...

PROMISE! PROMISE ON YOUR HONOR!

ALL RIGHT. I PROMISE.

BUT...

WAIT FOR ME! I'LL COME BACK!

PETER, IT WORKED!
I FOUND THEM!
IN THE HIDING PLACE
. . .

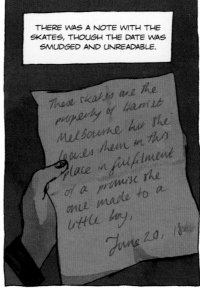

THERE WAS A NOTE WITH THE
SKATES, THOUGH THE DATE WAS
SMUDGED AND UNREADABLE.

These skates are the property of Harriet Melbourne but she leaves them in this place in fulfilment of a promise she once made to a little boy.

June 20, 18—

BUT I MADE MORE NOISE
THAN I SHOULD HAVE
DONE. A.G. GOT UP. I
PRETENDED TO BE ASLEEP
AND I WAITED . . .

IN THE END, I TRULY FELL ASLEEP.
I'D MISSED MY PRECIOUS CHANCE
OF GOING BACK TO THE GARDEN
THAT NIGHT.

WHILE A.G. WAS OUT SHOPPING,
I OILED THE SKATES.
I BORROWED SOME OLIVE
OIL FROM THE PANTRY.

PETER, I THINK THERE IS
NO THIRTEENTH HOUR. WHEN
THE CLOCK STRIKES THIRTEEN,
IT MEANS THAT FROM THAT
POINT THE HOURS DO NOT
EXIST IN ORDINARY TIME.

EVEN IF I STAY IN THE GARDEN
FOR MONTHS AND YEARS,
YOU CAN STILL EXPECT ME
BACK ON SATURDAY.

I WILL TRY IT OUT TONIGHT. I WILL
STAY A LONG TIME AND THEN COME
BACK. AND IF IT WORKS, THEN ON
FRIDAY NIGHT I WILL STAY . . .

. . . FOREVER IF
I CHOOSE.

PETER, WHAT A STRANGE NIGHT! IT STARTED WELL. I WENT OUT WITH THE SKATES, AND HATTY HAD HERS TOO. I HADN'T THOUGHT OF THAT. THERE SHOULD ONLY HAVE BEEN ONE PAIR . . .

HATTY WANTED TO SKATE ALL THE WAY TO ELY. STRANGELY, I COULD SKATE QUITE WELL. THOUGH NOT AS WELL AS HER. IT WAS A LONG WAY. BUT SHE WASN'T TIRED. AND NEITHER WAS I.

IN ELY, SHE WANTED TO CLIMB THE TOWER. IT WAS LATE. THERE WAS HARDLY ANYONE ELSE THERE.

BUT YOU KNOW THAT, DON'T YOU, PETER?

P . . . PETER?

HOW DID YOU DO IT?

BUT, TOM, WHERE'S THE GARDEN? I THOUGHT YOU WERE WITH HATTY, IN THE GARDEN. AND WHERE IS HATTY?

HERE! RIGHT OPPOSITE YOU!

BUT THAT'S NOT HATTY: THAT'S A GROWN-UP WOMAN!

SHE'S GROWN-UP!

WHO WAS HE? WHAT WAS HE? HE WAS LIKE YOU, AND HE WAS UNREAL-LOOKING, JUST LIKE YOU.

HE WAS MY BROTHER, PETER.

BUT HE'S REAL, HATTY. HE'S REAL, LIKE ME. YOU AGREED I WAS REAL, HATTY.

PETER, WHEN I GET HOME, TELL ME HOW YOU MANAGED TO BE THERE.

I WAS ASLEEP. I WAS DREAMING.

THEN IT STARTED TO GET DARK AND WE MET BARTY, SOMEONE HATTY KNEW.

HE SAID HE WOULD TAKE US BACK IN HIS HORSE AND GIG.

I HAD TO TALK TO HATTY. THERE WERE THINGS I NEEDED TO ASK HER BEFORE I DECIDED TO STAY IN THE GARDEN THAT EVENING.

BUT SHE WAS ONLY TALKING TO BARTY.

WORSE, SHE WAS BEHAVING AS IF SHE DID NOT REMEMBER ME — OR DID NOT SEE ME — OR BOTH.

NO! NOT THIS TIME! NOT NOW!

WHAT IS IT, TOM? HAVE YOU BEEN IN A NIGHTMARE? BUT, ANYWAY, IT'S OVER. WHY, HERE WE ARE ON FRIDAY MORNING, AND TOMORROW YOU'RE GOING HOME!

IT'S BECAUSE I LET MYSELF FALL ASLEEP IN THE GIG.

BUT TONIGHT I WILL GO BACK TO THE GARDEN.

FOR TIME IN THE GARDEN CAN GO BACK, AND SHE MAY BE A LITTLE GIRL AGAIN TONIGHT, AND WE SHALL PLAY GAMES TOGETHER.

I AM SURE I WILL BE HOME BEFORE YOU RECEIVE THIS LAST LETTER, BUT I WILL HAVE A WHOLE LIFE TO TELL YOU ABOUT. SEE YOU TOMORROW — AND IN A LONG, LONG TIME.

YOUR BROTHER TOM.

WELL, TOM, IT'S OUR LAST MEAL TOGETHER. WE SHALL MISS YOU . . .

I HOPE YOU'LL HAVE HAPPY MEMORIES OF YOUR STAY HERE.

DONGGG !

NO!

NO! NO!!

I AM GOING INTO THE GARDEN!

HATTY?

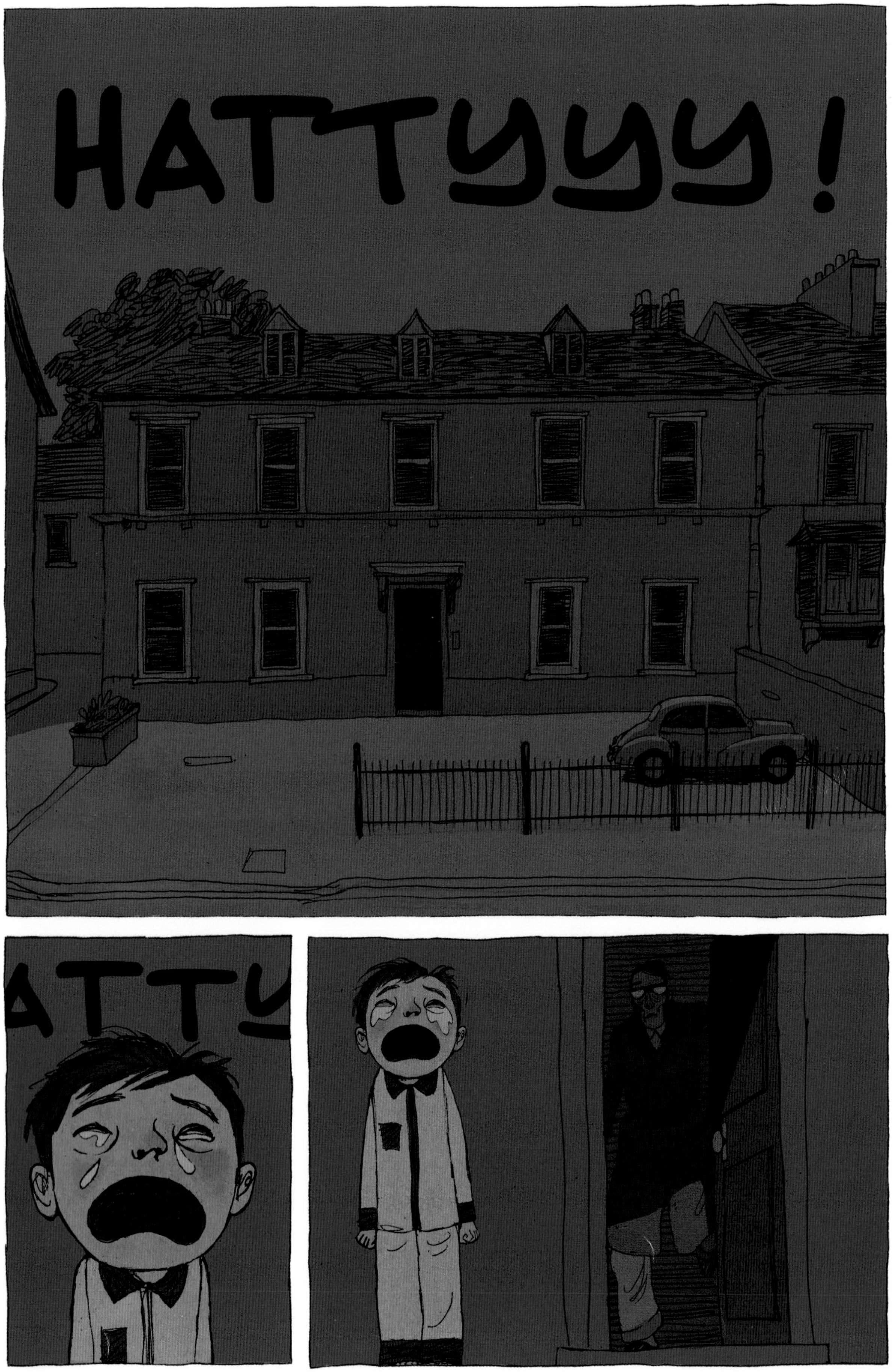
HATTYYY!
ATTY

I TOLD THE OTHER TENANTS HE WAS SLEEPWALKING.

AT LEAST I THINK HE WAS.

WE'LL APOLOGIZE TO MRS. BARTHOLOMEW TOMORROW.

I'LL GO AND SEE OLD MRS. BARTHOLOMEW.

SHE'S NOT HAPPY. SHE WANTS TOM HIMSELF TO GO TO HER.

I SHOULDN'T DREAM OF SENDING HIM! I SHALL TELL HER SO!

CAREFUL, GWEN! SHE IS THE LANDLADY. IF WE UPSET HER, SHE COULD BE VERY AWKWARD.

ALL THE SAME!

NO. I'LL GO TO HER. I OUGHT TO. I DON'T MIND.

I SHAN'T LET YOU, TOM!

I SHALL GO.

YES?

I'VE COME TO SAY I'M SORRY.

YOUR NAME'S TOM, ISN'T IT?

I'VE COME TO APOLOGIZE.

YOU'RE REAL: A REAL, FLESH-AND-BLOOD BOY . . . AND IN THE MIDDLE OF LAST NIGHT . . .

I'M SORRY ABOUT LAST NIGHT.

YOU SCREAMED OUT IN THE MIDDLE OF THE NIGHT: YOU WOKE ME.

I'VE SAID I'M SORRY.

YOU CALLED OUT. YOU CALLED A NAME.

OH, TOM, DON'T YOU UNDERSTAND? YOU CALLED ME: I'M HATTY.

THAT'S THE BAROMETER FROM THE MELBOURNES' HALL.

THAT'S YOUNG BARTY!

YES. A LIKENESS TAKEN SOON AFTER WE WERE MARRIED.

YOU MARRIED YOUNG BARTY?

YES, TOM.

I'M HATTY.

BUT HATTY WAS A GIRL WHEN QUEEN VICTORIA REIGNED.

I'M A VICTORIAN. WHAT IS ODD ABOUT THAT?

QUEEN VICTORIA CAME TO THE THRONE IN 1837.

BUT THAT WAS A LONG TIME BEFORE I WAS BORN. I WAS BORN TOWARDS THE END OF THE QUEEN'S REIGN.

BUT I DON'T UNDERSTAND! I DON'T UNDERSTAND! THE GARDEN GONE . . . AND YET THE BAROMETER HERE . . . AND YOU SAY YOU WERE HATTY . . .

WHAT HAPPENED AFTER THE DAY I SKATED TO ELY WITH HATTY — THE LAST TIME WE SAW EACH OTHER?

THE LAST TIME? BUT, NO, TOM, THAT WASN'T THE LAST TIME I SAW YOU. HAVE YOU FORGOTTEN?

YOU WERE HATTY!

YOU ARE HATTY!

YOU'RE REALLY HATTY!

IT WAS IN THE YEAR 1895, THAT YOU AND I, TOM, SKATED ALL THE WAY TO ELY: THE YEAR OF THE FAMOUS GREAT FROST. THAT DAY, ON THE WAY HOME FROM ELY, WE MET BARTY, AND HE GAVE US A LIFT.

I MARRIED BARTY THE FOLLOWING YEAR. DOING THE LAST OF MY PACKING ON THE EVE OF MY WEDDING DAY, I REMEMBERED MY SKATES, AND THAT MADE ME REMEMBER YOU, TOM. I'D KEPT THE SKATES WHERE I'D PROMISED YOU I WOULD, AND I KNEW THAT I HAD TO LEAVE THEM THERE, ALTHOUGH IT WAS SO LONG SINCE I'D SEEN YOU. I WROTE A NOTE OF EXPLANATION AND LEFT IT WITH THEM.

I FOUND IT. BUT THE DATE WAS SMUDGED.

THAT NIGHT WAS VERY HOT, SULTRY AND THUNDERY. I COULDN'T SLEEP. I THOUGHT OF MY WEDDING THE NEXT DAY, AND, FOR THE FIRST TIME, I THOUGHT OF ALL I WOULD BE LEAVING BEHIND ME: MY CHILDHOOD AND ALL THE TIMES I HAD SPENT IN THE GARDEN — IN THE GARDEN WITH YOU, TOM.

I WENT INTO AN EMPTY BEDROOM AT THE BACK OF THE HOUSE, OVERLOOKING THE GARDEN, A SPARE BEDROOM. I COULD SEE THE GARDEN LIT UP BY FLASHES OF LIGHTNING.

THEN I SAW YOU . . .

. . . WHEN THE STORM WAS AT ITS WORST. OH, TOM, IT WAS TERRIBLE TO SEE, WASN'T IT?

AND THEN I KNEW, TOM, THAT THE GARDEN WAS CHANGING ALL THE TIME, BECAUSE NOTHING STANDS STILL, EXCEPT IN OUR MEMORY.

AND WHAT HAPPENED NEXT?

BARTY AND I WERE MARRIED AND WENT TO LIVE ON ONE OF HIS FATHER'S FARMS IN THE FENS; AND WE WERE VERY HAPPY.

AND THEN?

HUBERT AND EDGAR BOTH LEFT THE HOUSE, AND JAMES CARRIED ON ALONE. THE BUSINESS WENT FROM BAD TO WORSE, AND IN THE END HE DECIDED TO EMIGRATE. BEFORE HE WENT, HE SOLD THE HOUSE.

BARTY AND I CAME OVER FOR THE AUCTION. THE HOUSE ALREADY LOOKED VERY DIFFERENT BY THEN. JAMES HAD BEEN SHORT OF MONEY, AND SO HE'D SOLD FIRST THE TWO MEADOWS, AND THEN THE ORCHARD, AND THEN EVEN THE GARDEN. THE GARDEN HAD QUITE GONE, AND THEY WERE BUILDING HOUSES AT WHAT HAD BEEN THE BOTTOM OF IT. NONE OF THE TREES WAS LEFT STANDING, EXCEPT TRICKSY. YOU CAN STILL SEE TRICKSY STANDING IN ONE OF THOSE GARDENS.

AT THE AUCTION, BARTY BOUGHT SOME OF THE FURNITURE THAT I FANCIED.

BUT YOU COULDN'T TAKE THE GRANDFATHER CLOCK AWAY WITH YOU INTO THE FENS.

IT NEVER NEEDED TO BE MOVED, FOR BARTY BOUGHT THE HOUSE — BUT HE SAID IT WASN'T A GENTLEMAN'S HOUSE ANY MORE, WITH NO GARDEN TO IT. HE MADE FLATS OUT OF IT, AND LET THEM.

THEN, MANY YEARS LATER, BARTY DIED. OUR TWO SONS HAD BEEN KILLED IN THE WAR. I WAS LEFT QUITE ALONE, SO I CAME HERE AND I'VE LIVED HERE EVER SINCE.

AND SINCE YOU'VE COME TO LIVE HERE, YOU'VE OFTEN GONE BACK IN TIME, HAVEN'T YOU?

GONE BACK IN TIME?

GONE BACK INTO THE PAST.

WHEN YOU'RE MY AGE, TOM, YOU LIVE IN THE PAST A GREAT DEAL. YOU REMEMBER IT; YOU DREAM OF IT.

BUT I HAVE TO SAY THAT NEVER BEFORE THIS SUMMER HAVE I DREAMED OF THE GARDEN SO OFTEN, AND NEVER BEFORE THIS SUMMER HAVE I REMEMBERED SO VIVIDLY WHAT IT FELT LIKE TO BE THE LITTLE HATTY — TO BE LONGING FOR SOMEONE TO PLAY WITH AND FOR SOMEWHERE TO PLAY.

BUT THOSE WERE THE THINGS I WANTED HERE, THIS SUMMER.

BUT THESE LAST FEW NIGHTS, BEFORE LAST NIGHT, YOU'VE HARDLY DREAMT OF THE GARDEN AT ALL; YOU'VE BEEN DREAMING OF WINTER AND SKATING.

YES, AND ALSO OF BARTY; I DREAMED LESS AND LESS OF THE GARDEN AND OF YOU, TOM.

I SUPPOSE YOU COULDN'T HELP THAT, IF YOU WERE GROWING UP.

YOU WERE GETTING THINNER — THINNER THROUGH — EVERY WINTER THAT I SAW YOU. BY THE END OF THAT DRIVE HOME WITH BARTY, YOU SEEMED TO HAVE VANISHED AWAY ALTOGETHER.

AND SO, LAST NIGHT . . .

LAST NIGHT I DREAMT OF MY WEDDING DAY AND OF GOING AWAY FROM HERE ALTOGETHER, TO LIVE IN THE FENS.

AND LAST NIGHT, WHEN I WENT DOWN AND OPENED THE GARDEN DOOR, THE GARDEN WASN'T THERE ANYMORE. THAT WAS WHEN I SCREAMED OUT.

YOU WOKE ME. I KNEW IT WAS TOM CALLING TO ME FOR HELP, ALTHOUGH I DIDN'T UNDERSTAND, THEN.

I COULDN'T BELIEVE YOU WERE REAL, UNTIL I SAW YOU THIS MORNING.

WE'RE BOTH REAL.

OF COURSE! AS IT'S WRITTEN ON THE CLOCK . . .

TIME NO LONGER!

DONG !

92

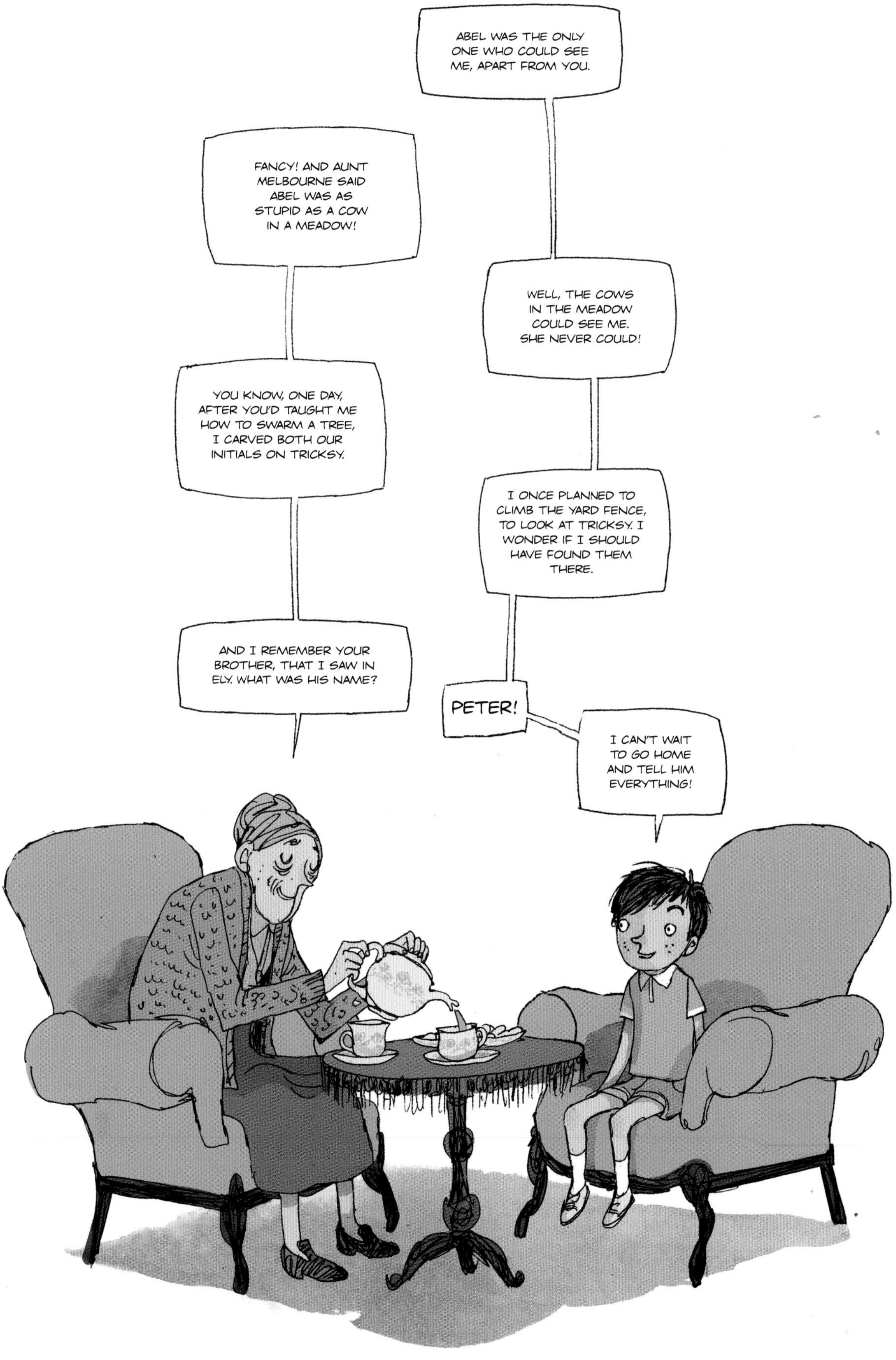
ABEL WAS THE ONLY ONE WHO COULD SEE ME, APART FROM YOU.
FANCY! AND AUNT MELBOURNE SAID ABEL WAS AS STUPID AS A COW IN A MEADOW!
WELL, THE COWS IN THE MEADOW COULD SEE ME. SHE NEVER COULD!
YOU KNOW, ONE DAY, AFTER YOU'D TAUGHT ME HOW TO SWARM A TREE, I CARVED BOTH OUR INITIALS ON TRICKSY.
I ONCE PLANNED TO CLIMB THE YARD FENCE, TO LOOK AT TRICKSY. I WONDER IF I SHOULD HAVE FOUND THEM THERE.
AND I REMEMBER YOUR BROTHER, THAT I SAW IN ELY. WHAT WAS HIS NAME?
PETER!
I CAN'T WAIT TO GO HOME AND TELL HIM EVERYTHING!

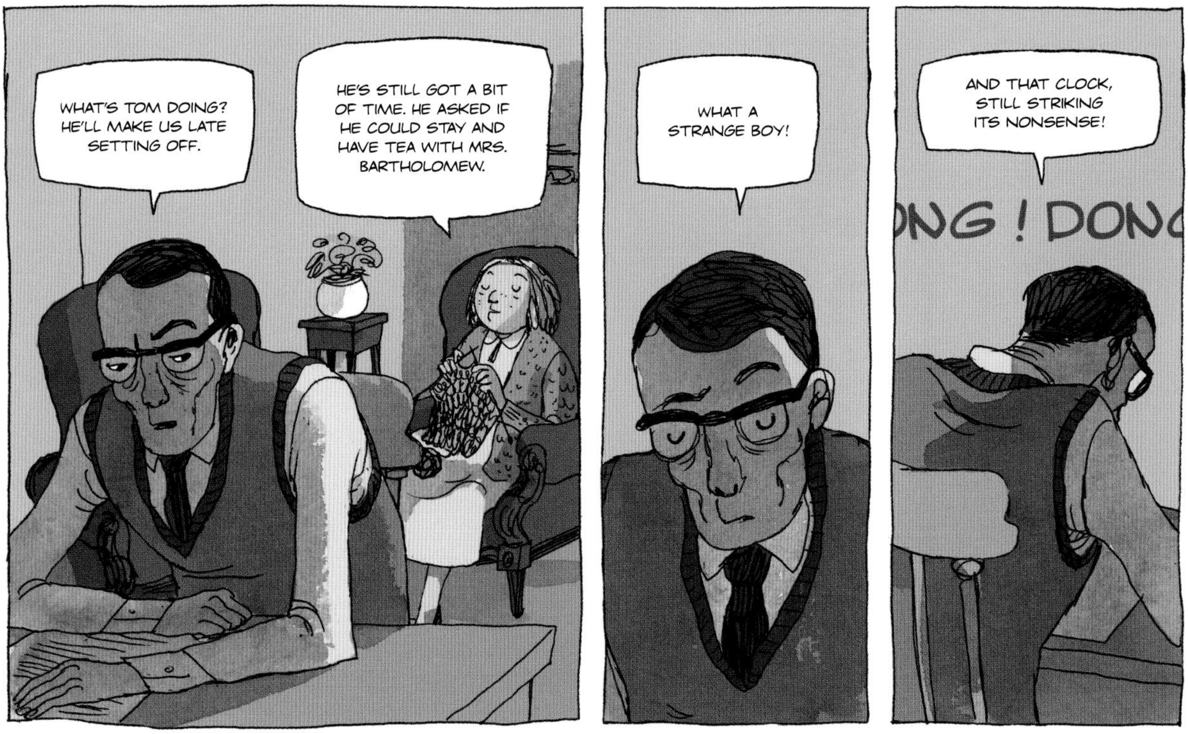
WHAT'S TOM DOING? HE'LL MAKE US LATE SETTING OFF.
HE'S STILL GOT A BIT OF TIME. HE ASKED IF HE COULD STAY AND HAVE TEA WITH MRS. BARTHOLOMEW.
WHAT A STRANGE BOY!
AND THAT CLOCK, STILL STRIKING ITS NONSENSE!
NG ! DONG

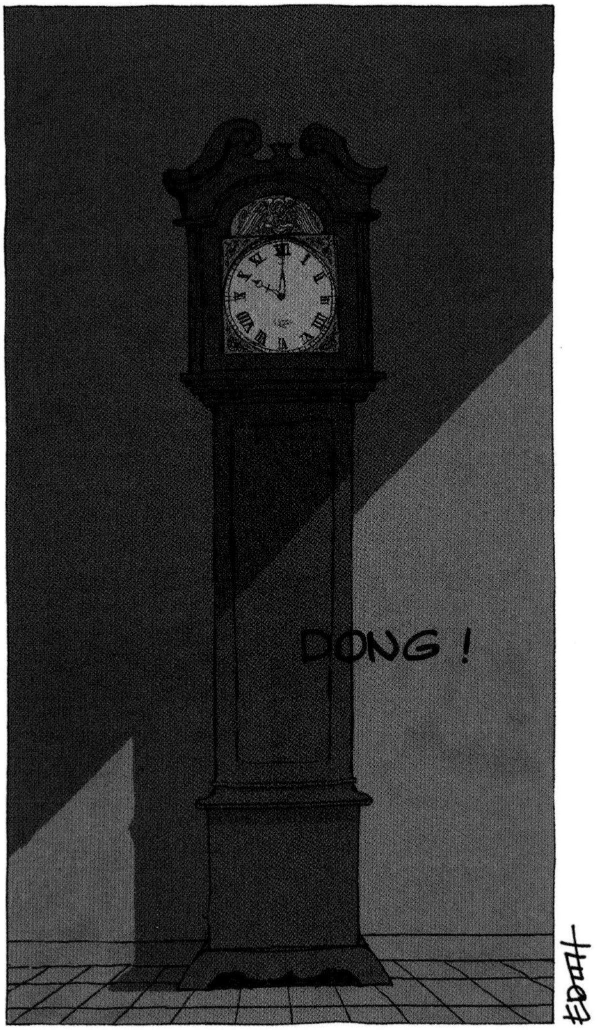
DONG !

15 August 2000

A small house, just south of Cambridge.

I'm a repeat-offender reader, guilty as charged. Over the past thirty years I've returned to *Tom's Midnight Garden* more times than I can remember. And now I'm here, at the home of Philippa Pearce, and I have to pinch myself to make sure I'm not dreaming. As we get up from lunch, chatting, I spy on a wall one of those old barometers set in an extravagantly-carved wooden surround, a favorite in middle-class homes of the early 1900s. In my studied English, I begin: "But . . . I recognize it, that barometer!" "You've a good memory," Philippa Pearce replies, with a little smile.

I appreciated the comment. That said, my memory here deserved little merit: having reread the book every year since I was eleven, I knew every detail like the back of my hand. But everything is there, in the memory. Good or bad.

In the wake of Marcel Proust and Virginia Woolf, it's impossible to ignore the fact that our remembrances are at the heart of creativity, and a story is the encrypted realization of an experience. Each of us has our own experiences, and our own way of processing them. For Philippa Pearce it is childhood—on both a personal and universal level—that has left a lasting impression on her writing.

Her work is filled with children, and with ghosts. Without doubt a very British literary tradition. But one to which Philippa Pearce conforms only in order to evoke, indirectly, the presence of a father who "survived" the Great War (probably returning shell-shocked). "My mother," she wrote to me, "had three brothers, two of whom fought in the same war. One came back blind, the other was killed." She went on: "I like a good ghost story, but I no longer expect them to make me believe in ghosts."

In the garden of Hatty and Tom, the ghosts are memories—not dreams—that overlap, and even they get a little confused: "You're dead! You're a ghost!" Tom says to Hatty, who replies, "No, you're the ghost. You're the one who's dead!" We are all a ghost to somebody, as long as that person remembers us.

And then there's our background. Philippa Pearce is amongst those who believe that we are shaped and—to a large extent—defined by the environment of our formative years: colors, materials, smells, sounds we love—they are all traces of our childhood, more or less refined over the years.

Philippa Pearce was living just a hundred meters from THE garden and her childhood home, which she had resolved to keep forever in her sight. Yes, it's true: THE garden actually exists! She took me there and my initial blissful feeling of actually "entering" a story (an illusion really, since the garden had well and truly existed for many years!) was superseded by another, more disturbing, feeling—that of stepping into another person's memory. It took her natural tenderness and love not to succumb to the pain of her ongoing grief (as any other might), but to transform it, through writing, into a precious world of fantasy and wonder.

And one last detail in the form of a simple metaphor.

Philippa Pearce's father was a miller and close by the house runs the ever-flowing river that drove the mill. King's Mill—as it is called—was destined to bridge the eternal flow of time, a constant source of memories . . . whether one's memory is good or bad.

Frédéric Bézian
celebrated French graphic novelist and
friend and compatriot of Edith

Love and thanks to Riff.
Edith

PHILIPPA PEARCE (1920–2006) is the beloved author of more than thirty books for children. Her award-winning books include *Tom's Midnight Garden*, winner of the Carnegie Medal, *Mrs. Cockle's Cat,* winner of the Kate Greenaway Medal, and *Minnow on the Say*, a Carnegie Medal finalist.

EDITH is an award-winning graphic artist and illustrator. She studied art at École Nationale Supérieure des Arts Décoratifs in Paris. She has illustrated nineteen graphic novels and more than ten books for children. She currently resides in Le Havre, France.

Tom's Midnight Garden:
A Graphic Adaptation of the Philippa Pearce Classic

Freely adapted from *Tom's Midnight Garden*, by Philippa Pearce,
copyright © 1958 by Oxford University Press
Le jardin de minuit, Edith
© Editions Soleil, 2015

First published in French, under the following title : *Le journal de minuit*, Edith
© Editions Soleil – 2015
First published in English in Great Britain in 2016 by Oxford University Press
First published in the United States in 2018 by Greenwillow Books

The rights of the author and illustrator have been asserted in accordance with the Copyright, Designs and Patents Act, 1988.

Translation of front and end matter by Helen Johnson
Translation of graphic novel by Liz Cross

Library of Congress Control Number: 2017953731

ISBN 978-0-06-269657-1 (hardback)
ISBN 978-0-06-269656-4 (paperback)

18 19 20 21 22 LEO 10 9 8 7 6 5 4 3 2 1
First Edition

 Greenwillow Books